"Would you ever have told me?

"Or would you have allowed my child to be born into this world," Franco continued quietly, "without ever knowing the identity of its father?"

Ruth felt her mouth go dry. "I thought I was doing the right thing."

"The *right* thing? Surely, as a vicar's daughter, you *must* know that the last thing you were doing was the *right thing!*"

"All right, then, the *best* thing. For…everyone…"

Relax and enjoy our fabulous series about
couples whose passion results in pregnancies...
sometimes unexpected! Of course, the birth of
a baby is always a joyful event, and we can
guarantee that our characters will become
besotted moms and dads—
but what happened in those nine months before?

Share the surprises, emotions, drama
and suspense as our parents-to-be come to terms
with the prospect of bringing a new life into the
world. All will discover that
the business of making babies brings with it
the most special love of all....

Our next arrival will be
Her Secret Pregnancy
by
Sharon Kendrick

On sale August 2001, Harlequin Presents #2198

Cathy Williams

THE BABY SCANDAL

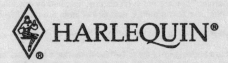

TORONTO • NEW YORK • LONDON
AMSTERDAM • PARIS • SYDNEY • HAMBURG
STOCKHOLM • ATHENS • TOKYO • MILAN • MADRID
PRAGUE • WARSAW • BUDAPEST • AUCKLAND

ISBN 0-373-12165-2

THE BABY SCANDAL

First North American Publication 2001.

Copyright © 2000 by Cathy Williams.

This edition published by arrangement with Harlequin Books S.A.

Visit us at www.eHarlequin.com

Printed in U.S.A.

CHAPTER ONE

RUTH heard the sound of footsteps striding up the staircase towards the offices and froze with a bundle of files in one hand. The wooden flooring, which was the final word in glamour, unfortunately had an annoying tendency to carry sound, and now, with the place completely deserted except for her, the amplified noise travelled with nerve-shattering precision straight to her wildly beating heart.

This was London.

She had laughed off all her parents' anxious concerns about the need to be careful in *The Big Bad City*, but now every word came flooding back to her with nightmarish clarity.

Muggers. Perverts. *Rapists*.

She cleared her throat and wondered whether she should gather up some courage and confront whoever had sneaked into the empty two-storey Victorian house, which had been tastefully converted one year ago to accommodate a staff of fifteen.

Courage, however, was not her forte, so she timidly stood her ground and prayed that the bloodthirsty, drug-driven maniac would see that there was nothing to steal and leave the way he had come.

The footsteps, which seemed to know precisely where they wanted to go, materialised into a dark shadow visible behind the closed glass door of the office. The corridor light had been switched off and, although it was summer, autumn was just around the corner, and at a little after seven-thirty night was already drawing in.

Now, she thought frantically, would be a very appropriate time to faint.

She didn't. Just the opposite. The soles of her feet appeared to have become glued to the floor, so that not only could she not collapse into a convenient heap to the ground, she couldn't even move.

The shadow pushed open the glass door and strode in with the typical aggressive confidence of someone with foul intent on his mind.

Some of her paralysed facial muscles came to life and she stuck her chin out bravely and said, in a high-pitched voice, 'May I help you?'

The man approaching her, now that she could see him clearly in the fluorescent light, was tall and powerfully built. He had his jacket slung over one shoulder and his free hand was rammed into the pocket of his trousers.

He didn't *look* like a crazed junkie, she thought desperately. On the other hand, he didn't look like a hapless tourist who had wandered accidentally into the wrong building, thinking it was a shop, perched as it was in one of the most exclusive shopping areas in London, between an expensive hat shop and an even more over-priced jeweller's.

In fact, there was nothing remotely hapless-looking about this man at all. His short hair was black, the eyes staring at her were piercingly blue and every angle of his face and body suggested a sort of hard aggression that she found overwhelming.

'Where is everyone?' he demanded, affording her a

brief glance and then proceeding to stroll around the office with proprietorial insolence.

Ruth followed his movements helplessly with her eyes.

'Perhaps you could tell me who you are?'

'Perhaps you could tell me who *you* are?' he said, pausing in his inspection of the assortment of desks and computer terminals to glance over his shoulder.

'I work here,' she answered, gathering up her failing courage and deciding that, since this man obviously didn't, then she had every right to be as curt with him as she wanted.

Unfortunately curt, like courage, was not in her repertoire. She was gentle to the point of blushingly gauche, and that was one of the reasons why she had moved to London. So that some of its brash self-confidence might somehow rub off on her by a mysterious process of osmosis.

'Name?'

'R-Ruth Jacobs,' Ruth stammered, forgetting that he had no business asking her anything at all, since he was a trespasser on the premises.

'Mmm. Doesn't ring any bells.' He had stopped inspecting the office now and was inspecting her instead, perched on the edge of one of the desks. 'You're not one of my editors. I have a list of them and your name isn't on it.'

Ruth was no longer terrified now. She was downright confused, and it showed in the transparent play of emotions on her smooth, pale face.

'Who *are* you?' she finally asked, lowering her eyes, because something about his blatant masculinity was a little too overpowering for her liking. 'I don't believe I caught your name.'

'Probably because I didn't give it,' he answered drily. 'Ruth Jacobs, Ruth Jacobs...' He tilted his head to one side and proceeded to stare at her with leisurely thoroughness. 'Yes, you could do...very well indeed...'

'Look...I'm in the process of locking up for the day...perhaps you could make an appointment to see Miss Hawes in the morning...?' It finally occurred to her that she must look very odd in this immobile position, with her hand semi-raised and holding a stack of files in a death-like grip. She unglued her feet from the ten-inch square they had occupied since the man entered the room, and darted across to Alison's desk for her appointment book.

'What's your job here?'

Ruth stopped what she was doing and took a deep breath. 'I refuse to answer any more questions until you tell me who you are,' she said in a bold rush. She could feel the colour redden her cheeks and, not for the first time, cursed her inability to dredge up even the remotest appearance of *savoir faire*. At the age of twenty-two, she should surely have left behind all this ridiculous blushing.

'I'm Franco Leoni.' He allowed a few seconds for his name to be absorbed, and when she continued to stare at him in bewilderment, he added, with a hint of impatience, 'I *own* this place, Miss Jacobs.'

''Oh,' Ruth said dubiously.

'Doesn't Alison tell you *anything*? Bloody awful man-management. How long have you been here? Are you a temp? Why the hell is she allowing a temp the responsibility of locking up? This is damned ridiculous.'

The rising irritation in his voice snapped her out of her zombie-like incomprehension.

'I'm not a temp, Mr Leoni,' she said shortly. 'I've been here virtually since it was taken over, eleven months ago.'

'Then you should know who I am. Where's Alison?'

'She left about an hour ago,' Ruth admitted reluctantly. She was frantically trying to recognise his name, and failing. She knew that the magazine, which had been a small, money-losing venture, had been taken over by some conglomerate or other, but the precise names of the people involved eluded her.

'Left for where? Get her on the line for me.'

'It's Friday, Mr Leoni. Miss Hawes won't be at home. I believe she was going out with…with…with her mother to the theatre.'

The small white lie was enough to bring another telling wash of colour to her face, and she stared resolutely at the bank of windows behind him. By nature she was scrupulously honest, but the convoluted workings of her brain had jumped ahead to some obscure idea that this man, whether he owned the place or not, might not be too impressed if he knew that her boss was on a dinner date with another man.

Alison, tall, vivacious, red-haired and thoroughly irreverent, was the sort of woman who spent her life rotating men and enjoying every minute of it. The last thing Ruth felt equipped to handle at seven-thirty on a Friday evening was a rotated boyfriend. And this man looked just the sort to appeal to her boss. Tall, striking, oozing sexuality. The sort of man who would appeal to most women, she conceded grudgingly, if you liked that sort of obvious look.

And if you were the type who didn't view basic good manners as an essential part of someone's personality.

'Then I suppose you'll just have to believe me when I tell you that I'm her boss, won't you?' He smiled slowly, watching her face as though amused by everything he could read there. 'And, believe it or not, I'm very glad that I bumped into you.' A speculative look had entered his eyes which she didn't much care for.

'I really need to be getting home…'

'Parents might be worried?'

'I don't live with my parents, *actually*,' Ruth informed him coldly. After nearly a year and a quarter, the novelty of having her own place, small and nondescript though it might be, was still a source of pleasure for her. She had been the last of her friends to fly the family nest and she had only done so because part of herself knew that she needed to.

She adored her parents, and loved the vicarage where she had lived since she was a child, but some obscure part of her had realised over the years that she had to spread her wings and sample what else the big world had to offer, or else buckle down to the realisation that her life would remain neatly parcelled up in the small village where she had grown up, surrounded by her cosy circle of friends all of whose ambitions had been to get married and have big families and never mind what else there was out there.

'No?' He didn't sound as though he believed that, and she glared at him.

'No. I'm twenty-two years old and I live in a flat in Hampstead. Now, do you want to make an appointment to see Miss Hawes in the morning or not?'

'You keep forgetting that I own this company. I'll see her in the morning, all right, but there's no need for me to make an appointment.'

Arrogant. That had been the word she'd been searching for to describe this man. She folded her arms and stared at him.

'Fine. Now perhaps you could see yourself to the door…?'

'Have you eaten?'

'What?'

'I said…'

'I heard what you said, Mr Leoni. I just wondered what you meant by it.'

'It means that I'm asking you to have dinner with me, Miss Jacobs.'

'I beg your pardon? I'm afraid…I couldn't possibly…I don't usually…'

'Accept dinner invitations from strangers?'

Yes, of course he had known what she had been thinking. She didn't have the knack of dissembling.

'That's right,' Ruth informed him, bristling. 'I know that must seem a little unusual to you, but I…' Where was she going with this one? A long monologue on her sheltered life? An explanation on being a vicar's daughter? Hadn't she come to London in the hope of gaining a bit of sophistication?

'I don't bite, Miss Jacobs.' He pushed himself away from the edge of the desk and she looked at him guardedly. If he was trying to make her believe that he was as harmless as the day was long, then he was living on another planet. Innocent and naïve she might be, but born yesterday she was not.

'You're my employee. Call it maintaining good relations with someone who works for me. Besides...' The assessing look was back on his face, sending little tingles of apprehension racing down her spine. 'I'd like to find out a bit more about you. Find out what you do in the company... And in case you still don't believe who I am...' He sighed and withdrew his wallet from his pocket, flicked it open and produced a letter to Alison, with his name flamboyantly emblazoned in black at the bottom, and his impressive title typed underneath.

Ruth scanned the letter briefly, noting in passing that it implied, with no attempts to beat around the bush, that the magazine had not accumulated enough sales and that it was time to get to the drawing board and sort it out. Presumably the very reason he had made an appearance at the ridiculous hour of seven-thirty on a Friday evening.

'There now,' he said, without the slightest trace of remorse that he had allowed her to wallow in nightmarish possibilities when he could have eliminated all that by simply identifying himself from the beginning. 'Believe me?'

'Thank you. Yes.'

'What do you do here?'

'Nothing very important,' Ruth said hastily, just in case he got it into his head that he could quiz her on the details of running a magazine. 'I'm an odd-job man...woman...person...I do a bit of typing, take calls, fetch and carry...that's all...'

'Tell me all about it over dinner.' His hand brushed

hers as he retrieved his letter and rammed it back into his pocket, and she could feel something inside her shrinking away from him. She had never met anyone quite like him before. Her boyfriends, all three of them, had been from her town, and they had been nice boys, the sort who were quite happy to trundle through life with modest aspirations and no great appetite for taking life by its head and felling it.

Franco Leoni looked the sort who relished challenges of that sort, thrived on them.

'Now, why don't we lock up here and find ourselves something to eat?' He was now so close to her that the hairs on the back of her neck were standing on end. Up close, he was even more disconcerting than he was with a bit of distance between them. Underneath the well-tailored clothes, every inch of his body spoke of well-toned, highly muscled power, and the impression was completed by his swarthy olive colouring, at odds with the strikingly light eyes.

She cautiously edged away and snatched her jacket from the hook on the wall and slipped it on.

'Good girl.' He opened the door for her and then watched as she nervously locked it behind her and shoved the jangling keyring into her bag.

'My car's just outside,' he said, as they walked down the staircase, 'and please, try not to wear that fraught expression on your face. It makes me feel like a sick old man who takes advantage of innocent young girls.' There was lazy amusement in his voice when he said this, and she didn't have to cast her eyes in his direction to know that he was laughing at her.

His car was a silver Jaguar. He opened the door for her, waited till she had shuffled inside, then strode to the driver's seat. As soon as the door was shut, he turned to her and said, 'Now, what do you fancy eating?'

'Anything!' Ruth said quickly. The darkness of the car made his presence even more stifling, and she cursed herself for having been railroaded into accepting his invitation. Yes, so he might well be the owner of the company she worked for, but that didn't mean that he was trustworthy where the opposite sex was concerned.

She wryly recognised the outdated prudery of her logic and smiled weakly to herself. As an only child, and a girl on top of it, she had been cherished and protected by her parents from day one.

'A girl without pretensions,' he murmured to himself, starting the engine, 'very refreshing. Don't care what you eat. Do you like Italian?'

'Fine. Yes.'

She could feel her heart pounding like a steam engine inside her as the car pulled smoothly away from the curb.

'So, where do you fit into the scheme of things at *Issues*?'

'If you own the magazine, how is it that you've never made an appearance there?' Ruth blurted out curiously. She was pressed against the car door and was looking at him warily with her wide grey eyes.

'The magazine is a very, very minor company of mine.' He glanced in her direction. 'Have I mentioned to you that I don't bite? I'm not infectious either, so there's no need to fall out of the car in your desperation to put a few more inches between us.' He looked back to the road and Ruth shuffled herself into a more normal position. 'I bought it because I thought it could be turned around and because I viewed it as a sort of hobby.'

'A sort of hobby?' Ruth asked incredulously. 'You bought a *magazine* as a *hobby*?' The thought of such extravagance was almost beyond comprehension. '*What sort of life do you lead?* I always thought that hobbies involved doing things like playing tennis, or squash or bird-watching...or collecting model railways...*Your hobby is buying small companies just for the fun of it?*'

'There's no need to sound quite so shocked,' he said irritably, frowning as he stared ahead and manoeuvred the honeycomb of narrow streets.

'Well, I *am* shocked,' Ruth informed him, forgetting to be intimidated.

'Why?'

'Because, Mr Leoni...'

'You can call me Franco. I've never been a great believer in surnames.'

'Because,' she continued, skipping over his interruption, 'it seems obscene to have so much money that you can buy a company just for the heck of it!'

'My little gesture,' he pointed out evenly, although a dark flush had spread across his neck, 'happens to have created jobs, and in accordance with the package I've agreed with all my employees, *including yourself*, you all stand to gain if the company succeeds.'

Ruth didn't say anything, and eventually, he said abruptly, 'Well? What have you got to say to that?'

'I...nothing...'

He clicked his tongue in annoyance. '*I...nothing...*' he mimicked. 'What does that mean? Does it mean that you have an opinion on the subject? You had one a minute ago…'

'It means that you're my employer, Mr Leoni…

'Franco!'

'Yes, well…'

'Say it!' he said grimly.

'Say what?'

'My name!'

'It means that you're my employer, Franco…' She went hot as she said that, and hurriedly moved on. 'And discretion is the better part of valour.' That was one of her father's favourite sayings. He spent so much time listening to his parishioners that he had always lectured to her on the importance of hearing without judging, and taking the wise course rather than the impulsive, thoughtless one.

'Hang discretion!'

Ruth looked at him curiously. Was he getting hot under the collar? He hadn't struck her as the sort of man who ever got hot under the collar.

'Okay,' she said soothingly, 'I take your point that you've created jobs, and if it succeeds then we all succeed. It just seems to me that *buying a company as a bit of fun* is the sort of thing…' She took a deep breath here and then said in a rush, 'That someone does because they have too much money and might be…bored…'

'*Bored?*' he spluttered furiously, swerving the car into a space by the pavement as though only suddenly remembering the purpose of the trip in the first place had been to get them to a restaurant, which he appeared to have overshot. He killed the engine and turned his full attention on her.

Ruth reverted to her original position against the car door. Her shoulder-length vanilla-blonde hair brushed the sides of her face and her mouth was parted in anticipation of some horrendous verbal attack, full frontal, no holds barred. He certainly looked in the mood for it.

He inhaled deeply, raked his fingers through his hair and then shook his head in wonderment. 'How long is it since I met you?' He glanced at his watch while Ruth helplessly wondered where this was going. 'Forty-five minutes? Forty-five minutes and you've managed to prod me in more wrong places than most people can accomplish in a lifetime.'

'I'm—I'm sorry...' Ruth stammered.

'Quite an achievement,' he carried on, ignoring her mumbled apology.

'I don't consider it much of an achievement to antagonise someone,' she said, aghast at his logic.

'Which is probably why you're so good at it.' He had regained his temporarily misplaced composure and clicked open his door. 'I'm looking forward to dinner,' he said, before he slid out of the driver's seat. 'This is the first time I've walked down a road and not known where it was leading.'

What road? Ruth thought, *as she stepped out of the car onto the pavement. What was he talking about?* She hoped that he didn't expect her to be some kind of cabaret for him, because she had no intentions of fulfilling his expectations, employer or not.

The Italian restaurant was small and crowded and smelled richly of garlic and herbs and good food. It was also familiar to the man at her side, because he was greeted warmly by the door and launched into fluent Italian, leaving her a chance to look around her while her mind churned with questions about him.

'You speak fluent Italian,' she said politely, as they were shown to their table. 'Have you lived in England long?'

They sat down and he stared at her thoughtfully. 'You look much younger than twenty-two. Where are you from?'

Ruth had spent her life being told that she looked much younger than she was. She supposed that by the time she hit fifty she would be glad for the compliment, but right now, sitting opposite a man who bristled with worldly-wise sophistication, it didn't strike her as much of a compliment.

'A very small town in Shropshire,' she said, staring at the menu which had been handed to her. 'You wouldn't have heard of it.'

'Try me.'

So she did, and when he admitted that he had never heard of the place she gave her shy, soft laugh and said, 'Told you so.'

'So you came here to London...for excitement?'

She shrugged. 'I fancied a change of scenery,' she said vaguely, not wanting to admit that the search for a bit of excitement had contributed more than a little to her reasons for leaving.

'And what were you doing before you moved here?' He hadn't bothered to look at the menu, and when the waiter came to take their orders, she realised that he already knew what he wanted. Halibut, grilled. Her choice of chicken in a wine and cream sauce seemed immoderate in comparison, but a lack of appetite was not something she had ever suffered from, despite her slight build. She had eaten her way through twenty-two years of her mother's wonderful home cooking, including puddings that ignored advice on cholesterol levels, and had never put on any excess weight.

'Secretarial work,' she answered. 'Plus I helped Mum and Dad a lot at home. Doing typing for Dad, going to see his parishioners...'

'Your father's a...priest?' He couldn't have sounded more shocked if she had said that her father manufactured opium for a living.

'A vicar,' she said defensively. 'And a brilliant one at that.'

He smiled, a long, warm smile that transformed his face, removed all the aggression, and sent little shivers scurrying up and down her spine like spiders.

'You're a vicar's daughter.'

'That's right.'

'Your parents must have had a fit when you told them that you wanted to move to London.'

He was watching her as though she was the most fascinating human being on the face of the earth, and the undiluted attention addled her brain and brought more waves of pink colour to her cheeks.

'They were very supportive, as a matter of fact.'

'But worried sick.'

'A little worried,' Ruth admitted, nervously playing with the cutlery next to her plate and then sticking her hands resolutely on her lap when she realised that fiddling was not classed as great restaurant etiquette.

'So...' The speculative look was back in his eyes as he relaxed in the chair and looked at her. 'Let me get this straight... You worked as a secretary after you left school, lived at home with your parents and then moved to London where you…did what until you started working at the magazine?'

'I found somewhere to live… Actually, Mum and Dad came with me a month before I left home and made sure that I had somewhere to go…I think they imagined me walking the streets of London and sleeping rough on park benches…' She smiled again, the same slow smile that transformed the features of her pretty but not extraordinary face into a quite striking glimpse of ethereal beauty.

'I got work temping at an office in Marble Arch and after a few months, when I was hunting around for something more permanent…' she shrugged and reflected on her stroke of luck '…I happened to be in the agency when Alison, Miss Hawes, arrived to register a job for a dogsbody, and I was given the job on the spot.'

'So you run errands,' he murmured to himself. 'And you're satisfied with that line of work?'

'Well, I do enjoy working for the magazine,' Ruth said thoughtfully, 'and hopefully I might be given some more responsibility when my appraisal comes up…the pay's very good, though…'

'I know. I've handled enough businesses to know that motivation and loyalty are heavily tied in to working conditions, and good pay makes for a good employee, generally speaking.'

Their food arrived and they both sat back to allow the large circular plates to be put in front of them.

'How many businesses do you own?' Ruth asked faintly.

'Sufficient to allow me very little free time, hence my non-appearance at the magazine. I spend most of my time out of the country, overseeing my divisions in North America and the Far East, although I *have* been to see how Alison was getting on a couple of times. You weren't there. I would have remembered you.'

Ruth, more relaxed now that she had something aside from him to concentrate on—namely the brimming plate of divine food in front of her—lowered her eyes and said to her forkful of chicken and vegetables, 'No, you wouldn't. I'm not one of life's memorable women.' Her parents had always told her that she was beautiful, but then all parents said stuff like that. She only had to look in the mirror to know that she simply wasn't flamboyant enough ever to cross the line between being reasonably pretty and downright sexy. She couldn't be sexy if she tried.

He didn't say anything.

Unusually for him, he was finding it hard to keep his eyes away from the woman sitting opposite him, her soft face downturned as she tucked into her food without inhibition.

He couldn't remember the last time he had been in the company of a woman who still had the capacity to blush. They could laugh, they could flirt, and they were adept at revealing enough of their bodies to incite interest, but when it came to the hesitant air of innocence that this woman in front of him possessed, they none of them could have captured it if they tried.

And it was this dreamy, uncertain shyness that had aroused him almost from the minute he had clapped eyes on her. He broke off to eat a mouthful of food, but his eyes slid back to her face of their own volition.

He had a ridiculous urge to impress her. To say

something or do something that would make her look at him with the hot interest he had become accustomed to in members of the opposite sex. He watched the way her blonde straight hair slipped across her face as she ate and the way she tucked it casually behind her ears. She looked about bloody sixteen! He must be going mad!

'You never told me,' she said, interrupting his thoughts, which were veering off wildly into the arena of sexual foreplay. 'Are you from Italy?' She blushed and smiled. 'Silly question. Of course you are with a name like yours. How long have you lived in London?'

'Most of my life. My mother was Irish, my father was Italian.' What, he wondered, would it feel like to reach out and touch that peach-smooth face? The thought fascinated him. He realised that he wasn't eating and shovelled some mouthfuls in while his mind wandered away again. What would her body look like? It was difficult to tell underneath her demure calf-length skirt and neat white blouse. He toyed with the fantasy of divesting her of both, very, very, very slowly, and he could feel himself stiffening at the thought of it.

This was ludicrous! He was responding like a teenager who had never touched a woman in his life before!

'How exotic!' she responded, and it occurred to him that, however damned exotic she might find his ancestry, it wasn't quite enough to distract her from the business of eating. In fact, he thought with a twitch of resentment, she seemed a lot more interested in the food than she did in him.

'There's no need to show polite interest,' he said abruptly, and her grey eyes registered dismay at his reaction.

'I *am* interested,' she protested, unnerved by the sudden brusqueness in his voice. She was boring him. Of course she was. How could a gauche woman like herself ever hope to capture the interest of a man like him, all glamour and fast-lane living. 'The food's wonderful, isn't it?' she volunteered tentatively, feeling her way towards a topic that might smooth the undercurrent that seemed to have inexplicably developed.

'I can see that you've enjoyed it,' he said wryly.

Ruth gave a sheepish smile. 'I have a very unladylike appetite, I'm afraid.' She had managed to eat every mouthful, and if she had been in the company of anyone else would have happily bolted down some dessert as well. Instead, she closed her knife and fork, declined pudding and accepted coffee.

'I guess you read what was in that letter I sent to your boss,' he said casually, eyeing her over the rim of his cup. He had pushed himself away from the table so that he could sit at an angle, crossing his long legs.

'Not really,' Ruth answered. 'I mean I scanned it…'

'But still managed to get a pretty good idea of what I was trying to say.'

'I don't think that Alison would approve of my discussing something that was meant for her eyes only,' Ruth eventually told him.

'I shouldn't trouble your head with such concerns,' he dismissed. 'I intend to have a little talk to the entire staff. Sales have picked up since we took over, but not enough. I've read what the three journalists have written over the months...have you?'

'Oh, yes,' Ruth said enthusiastically.

'And...? What's your verdict?'

She couldn't quite understand why her opinion should be of any concern, considering her lowly status in the company, but there was an interested glint in his eyes, so she sighed and said slowly, 'I think it's all been good. But I suppose there's a little element of having lost the way. I mean,' she said hurriedly, 'their articles are so varied that there's a bit of doubt as to what sector of the market the magazine is supposed to appeal to. Not,' she felt compelled to add, 'that I'm in any position to criticise.'

'Why not?' he asked bluntly, leaning forward so that his elbow was resting on the table and his eyes bored into her like skewers.

'Because I'm not an editor.'

'But you care about the company enough to want to see it improve?'

'Of course I do!' When she had joined it had been a fledgling firm, and was even now, and consequently, loyalty was abundantly given by everyone who worked in it.

'Enough to do your little bit?' he asked, leaning forward yet further.

'Naturally I do my best... I can't write, if that's what you mean...but I help out...' She looked at him, bewildered.

'Good! Just what I wanted to hear.' He signalled for the bill but kept his eyes on her face. 'Because I have a proposition to put to you...'

'What?' There was enough of a predatory expres-

sion on his face to give her a clue that whatever he
had in mind was not going to be to her liking.

'I'll discuss it with Alison first, but, yes…it's time
for a few changes, and you could be right where it
matters…'

CHAPTER TWO

WHEN she arrived at work the following Monday morning, it was to find Alison in her office, door shut, which was a rare phenomenon, and, even rarer still, an atmosphere of hushed efficiency amongst the staff who had managed to pole up for work at a quarter to eight—an hour before their due starting time on a Monday, this was always limited to a handful, which increased as the week progressed.

She walked across to Janet Peters, one of the editors, opened her mouth to ask what was going on and, before she could get the question out, was greeted with a series of facial movements and twitches that left her a little confused.

'Are you feeling all right, Jan?' Ruth asked, concerned, and in reply Janet crooked her finger for Ruth to lean forward,

'Guess who's in with Alison...' she hissed. 'Hence the unnatural deathly quiet in this place...'

'Franco Leoni, owner of *Issues*?' Ruth hazarded, and then grinned when Janet fell backwards in her chair and stared at her with profound consternation.

'How did you know?'

'I knew...because...I am possessed of strange mystic forces that leave me with the uncanny ability to *see into the other realm*.' She giggled and played with the blunt edge of one of her plaits, a sensible hairstyle that kept her hair away from her face though unfortunately made her look no older than twelve.

'Be serious!' Janet said sternly, by which time they had been joined by three others and the atmosphere was drifting inexorably back into cheerful, noisy confusion.

'How *did* you know?' Jack Brady asked, sitting on the desk and giving her a frank and open stare. Jack Brady, who looked only slightly older than twelve himself, with his freckles and thick fair hair, specialised in frank and open stares which fooled no one but the uninitiated.

'He came here on Friday night, just as I was about to leave. Scared me to death as a matter of fact.'

'Was that,' Jack asked, frowning and tilting his head to one side, 'before or after he asked you to lie prone on the desk so that he could have his wicked way with you?'

'Before,' Ruth said with a serious face. 'I felt fine afterwards.'

'Ruth Jacobs!' Jack said, shocked. 'You're not *supposed to say naughty things like that*! Especially looking the way you do, all fetching, sexy innocence with those two blonde pigtails and big, tempting eyes...' He playfully pulled the ends of both the plaits with his hands, so that she was more or less compelled to incline her body towards his, and it was while they were in this awkward stance, both of them laughing, that Alison's door opened and there was a general flurry of scattered bodies as Franco stood and watched what was going on.

Ruth and Jack were the last to detach themselves from the situation.

'An office hard at work,' Franco said, pushing himself away from the doorframe and strolling towards them with the friendly expression of a barracuda on the prowl for food. 'Such a reassuring thing to see—especially when I have just finished having a meeting with your boss to work out why the magazine isn't doing as well as it should.'

He was dressed in a silver-grey suit, which he managed to transform into something elegant rather than functional, and a pale blue and white shirt with a dark blue tie. Very conservative, very traditional yet, on him, shockingly attractive.

Jack, who had been reduced to a state of tongue-tied embarrassment, launched himself into a comprehensive stream of apologies, which Franco, not bothering to look at him at all, waved aside.

He somehow managed to turn his broad back on the assembled eight members of staff now busily working at their desks, heads down, eyes focused, so that he could devote every scrap of uninvited attention to Ruth, who was the last one left still standing and with nowhere to conceal herself.

'So,' he said softly, which just succeeded in making his exclusion of the rest of the office from their conversation all the more complete, 'does flirting list among your dogsbody jobs?'

'I wasn't...flirting!' Ruth protested in a low, heated voice. 'Jack was just...'

'Playing with your hair...'

She tried to slide her eyes around him to see whether their tête-à-tête was being observed, but decided that she would rather not know.

'That's r-right...' she stammered absent-mindedly,

as her eyes flitted over the downturned heads and rapt faces staring at computer screens.

He clicked his tongue impatiently, 'Would you mind looking at me when I'm talking to you?' he snapped, sharply enough for her to literally jump to attention.

'Of course!' She nearly saluted, and then had to stifle a giggle at the thought of what his expression would be like if she dared do any such thing.

'Do you recall our little conversation on Friday?'

'Which bit?' Ruth asked cautiously. Her smoky grey eyes wandered away as she tried to recall what they had spoken about. She knew that if she put her mind to it she would have no trouble at all, although the overwhelming impression that remained with her of that night, like a thorn driven deep into her side, was the unwelcome feeling of being bludgeoned into the ground by something much like a steamroller.

'Could I have your attention?' he asked in a grim, irritable voice, and she shot him a nervous smile in response.

Did he realise that he had just raised his voice one or two decibels, and that in the small office all those downcast eyes were quietly boring a hole in the back of his neck, and that all those subdued voices would be eagerly anticipating his departure so that they could lay into her with a thousand and one questions?

Having never been the focus of gossip, the thought of it now was enough to bring Ruth out in a cold sweat.

She could hardly tell him to lower his tone, though, so she compensated by reducing the level of hers so much that he had to bend down to hear what she was saying.

'I *am* paying attention, to every word you're saying,' she whispered furtively, feeling like a dodgy character in a third-rate movie.

'I've spoken to Alison about my little proposition...'

'What little proposition?'

'Do you have *any* concentration span *at all*?' he snapped.

He glared down at her. Most of the women he knew—had ever known, for that matter—achieved a near perfect complexion through generous, skilful application of make-up. This girl, staring up at him, her teeth anxiously worrying her lip, had the most perfect complexion he had ever clapped eyes on, without the aid of any make-up at all. God, he could feel his mind beginning to drift, *again*, and he glared even more ferociously at her, further maddened by the glaringly obvious fact that although she was hearing every belligerent word he was saying she wasn't seeing *him* at all.

Who was that boy who had been playing with her hair? Was there something going on there?

He fought to impose a bit of self-control and managed a stiff, artificial smile which appeared to alarm the object of his attentions even more than his aggression had done a minute before.

'Maybe we could continue this conversation in Alison's office. A bit more private.'

'Oh, yes!' Ruth breathed a sigh of relief. She had just managed to accidentally catch Jack's eye and had quickly looked away when he had grinned and winked at her.

'After you,' he said, stepping aside so that she could precede him.

Ruth, in her usual uninspiring attire of neat powder-blue skirt and long-sleeves blouse, was acutely conscious of his eyes behind her, following her movements. She was also conscious of Jack shooting her telling, questioning looks from where he was seated at an angle away from his desk, and with a sidelong glance she smiled at him and flashed him the smallest of waves. A conspiratorial wave that combined bewilderment at Franco Leoni's inexplicable shepherding of her into Alison's office and dread at what it indicated.

'Mind if I have a word with Ruth alone?' Franco asked, as soon as they were in the office, and Alison obligingly exited at speed, either relieved to be out of his presence or else frantic to obey his every command.

'Take a seat.' He indicated the black chair in front of the desk and Ruth sat down, only to find that he had remained standing, so that to look at him she had to crane her neck.

He strolled across to the bay window which opened onto the busy view of a London street in full swing, and, after idly staring out for a few seconds, he turned to face her, relaxing against the windowsill, arms folded.

'I won't be telling you anything that the rest of your colleagues will not hear for themselves very shortly, but the gist of my chat with Alison concerns what we briefly discussed last Friday evening. The magazine seems to have found itself in something of a rut. As you rightly pointed out, neither one thing nor another.'

Ruth felt a sudden warm glow at the unexpected compliment.

'We have three talented reporters with good, solid styles of writing, but their subject matter is too disparate. Sport, fashion, natural disasters. Are you following me?'

'Of course I'm following you. I'm not a complete idiot, you know!' She felt a sudden flash of anger at his patronising attitude. Why had he called her in on her own to give this little speech? He hadn't made it clear, unless it was to sack her, but she couldn't really see why he would do that. Her contribution had nothing to do with the actual running of the magazine. She was a gofer, and a pretty good one at that, with lots of enthusiasm.

No, the only reason she could see for this one-to-one chat was to given him a chance of shooting down everything she said in flames. Maybe her soft nature was just too much of a temptation for a man like him. He simply couldn't resist walking over her.

However soft she was, Ruth had no intention of being walked over. When pushed, there was a stubborn streak in her that made her dig her heels in and refuse to budge.

'Sorry,' he said, with a shadow of a smile. The apology, so unexpected, was enough to pull her down a peg or two, and she responded helplessly to the sincerity in his voice.

'That's okay,' she said with a half-smile, lowering her eyes and then belatedly realising that all this timidity was no way to deal with this man. She looked at him fully and he stared back at her in silence for a few seconds.

'I don't suppose you were familiar with the magazine before we took it over?'

Ruth shook her head.

He went to the desk, but instead of sedately sitting on the chair he perched on the surface of the desk, so that he was still staring down at her—though from a lesser height, and infinitely closer.

'It failed because there simply wasn't enough money to pay any half-respectable reporter, and as a result, the articles were shallow and superficial. But, as far as I am concerned, the essence of the magazine was good. It dealt solely with topical problems. Drugs in the schoolyard, corruption in local politics, that sort of thing.'

'Oh. Yes,' Ruth said faintly, wondering what this had to do with her.

'I think we need to drag it back to that formula, but handle it better than our predecessors.'

'What does Alison think of your idea?' Ruth asked, leaning forward to rest the palms of her hands on her knees and staring up at him.

The pigtails were a mistake. She had not expected to be confronted with Franco Leoni first thing in the morning or else she would have tried for a more sophisticated look. She could tell from the way that he looked at her that he was finding it difficult not to click his tongue impatiently at the image she presented.

'Oh, she agrees entirely,' he said. 'In fact, she's probably out there explaining all of this to your colleagues...' he looked at her for a fraction longer than necessary '…and friends,' he ended on a soft note, which made Ruth frown.

'Well, I hope you don't mind my asking, but why have you taken me to one side to explain all this when I could have been out there hearing it along with everyone else?'

'Because…' He inclined his head to one side and, worryingly, appeared to give the question quite a bit of thought. 'Because there's a further little matter I wanted to discuss with you…'

'What?' She inadvertently stiffened at the tone in his voice.

'I think you could be a great deal of help in getting this magazine back on the straight and narrow.'

'Me…?' Ruth squeaked. She almost burst out laughing at that, and managed to contain the urge in the nick of time.

If he thought that she was, mysteriously, a wonderful and gifted reporter labouring under the disguise of a dogsbody, then he was way off target. The most she had ever written were essays at school, and she'd occasionally helped her dad to write the odd sermon for Sunday's congregation.

Hard-hitting articles on topical issues were quite outside her realm of capability.

'Yes, you. And there's no need to sound so shocked. Don't you have any faith in your abilities?'

'I couldn't write to save my life!'

'Why not? Have you ever tried?' There was curiosity etched on his dark, handsome face as he leant a little closer towards her while she continued to stare at him with frank disbelief.

'Of course I have,' Ruth said firmly, 'at school. I

managed to get my A level in English, but I certainly wouldn't want to put it to the test by writing an article. And I fancy,' she said with a slow smile, 'that not very many readers would thank me for the effort either.'

'So you never considered university?'

Ruth eyed him warily, wondering what this had to do with anything.

Franco, leaning towards her, felt his eyes stray to the blunt edges of her plaits, and he wondered what she would do if he took them and tugged at them, the way the boy in the office had. She certainly wouldn't respond with laughter. Apprehension, more like it. The thought generated another surge of hot antagonism towards the young lad who was clearly on familiar enough terms with her to touch her hair, play with it.

Were they sleeping together?

He would find out. He would make it his business to find out. In fact, he would make it his business to find out everything he possibly could about this girl sitting in front of him, if only to sate his gnawing curiosity.

He felt another urge to *make her notice him*, and scowled at such an adolescent response.

'No,' she laughed. 'I'm no brainbox. My only virtues are that I'm enthusiastic and I'm prepared to work hard.'

'Really?' he drawled. 'Admirable virtues, I must say.' His blue eyes lingered on her face, which turned crimson in response as the ambiguity of his observation sank in. 'You blush easily. Is that because I make you feel uncomfortable?' He was staring at her so fixedly that Ruth disengaged her eyes from his face. A fatal mistake, because as they travelled the length of his body, they came to his hands, resting casually over his thighs. Just a couple of inches higher and she could discern, beneath the fine silk of his trousers, the faint but unmistakable bulge of his manhood. The sight of it made her feel a little faint.

'No,' she denied quickly, staring back into his blue eyes. 'I blush with everyone…no discrimination there, I'm afraid…I'm just hopeless when it comes to that kind of thing. Anyway, you never said what you wanted to talk to me about…'

'Oh, didn't I?'

'No,' she said drily, 'you didn't.'

He flashed her a smile. 'Perhaps that's because I've been beating about the bush trying to think of how best I can put my suggestion to you. And, before you ask, it has nothing to do with writing articles for the magazine.'

'Then what?'

'Like I said to you, I think we need to get back to hard-hitting articles, the sort of stories that people are interested in and can identify with.' He rubbed his chin thoughtfully with his finger, then stood up and began pacing through the room, as though his brain needed the physical movement to work clearly. 'And I intend to lead by example.'

'Oh?' Ruth felt like someone who had accidentally strayed into a maze and was in the process of getting more and more lost.

'I intend to tackle the first article myself—get a feel for what's out there and what our best vantage point is when it comes to reporting it…'

'I thought you were a businessman,' Ruth said,

aware that she must have missed something vital but not too sure what it could be.

'I have lots of strings to my bow,' he murmured, waiting for her to ask for clarification and then disproportionately irked when she simply nodded and informed him that diving in the deep end and doing some reporting himself sounded a very good idea to her.

'Was that your intention when you bought the magazine?' she asked, and he frowned his incomprehension at her question. 'I mean,' she elaborated slowly, 'to get involved in the reporting side of things. Must make quite a change from working in an office...'

'I don't *work in an office*!' he growled. 'I *run companies*.'

'I know. But from the inside of an office.'

'Yes, admittedly, I *have a desk*, and all the usual accoutrements of my trade, but...'

'I'm sorry, I didn't mean to be rude.'

He muttered something inaudible under his breath and wondered how on earth he could have such chokingly erotic fantasies about someone whose eyes barely rested on him long enough to establish that he was a man. Never mind an immensely rich and powerful one.

'I just wondered,' she ploughed on, 'whether your decision to get involved has to do with your boredom at the office...'

This time the indecipherable noise was somewhat louder and more alarming.

'I'm sorry,' Ruth said a little desperately, wondering how she had managed to put both feet in it with such apparent ease. 'I forgot. You don't work at an office.

Well, you more or less own the office, and you're not bored. I'm sorry. I don't know why I said what I did. I must be tired. It's been an awfully tiring weekend.'

'Has it? Doing what, Ruth?' he asked slyly. 'Are you and that boy out there involved? Because I tell you from now that I don't encourage office romances. The first thing to suffer is usually the work.'

'What?' Ruth asked, appalled at his sweeping assumptions. How had they swerved off onto this topic anyway? She thought that they had been discussing his idea to do a spot of reporting. Now here they were on the subject of her personal life, and her non-existent love-life at that.

'I asked you whether—'

'I heard you! No! Of *course* not! Jack and I are friends! I wouldn't dream of... *No*...'

Franco tried not to smile with satisfaction. He couldn't have explained why, but from the minute he had come upon the two of them in the office, clearly at ease with one another, he had been determined to find out what was going on. The surprise on her face at the thought of being romantically involved with the boy was enough to persuade him of the honesty of her reply.

In some part of him he could feel that this was getting out of hand. Mild interest was fine, but she was getting under his skin, making him want more of her... He shifted his position and abruptly sat down, because his body was responding to her with its now familiar obstinate refusal to obey the commands of his head.

'Good, because for what I have in mind romantic involvement is not such a good idea.' He glanced up at her and asked casually, 'You're not involved with anyone, are you? I mean, no lovers on the scene?' He knew that he was shamelessly exploiting his situation, taking advantage of his position to prise answers out of her that he wanted to know and she, quite possibly, did not want to reveal, but he blithely squashed any guilt.

'No!' Her face was flushed and she fought down her instinctive embarrassment at his forthrightness to say, somewhat belatedly, 'And you have no right to ask me questions like that. What I do in my private life is...'

'I know, I know...' he said, ready to apologise now that he had heard what he needed to know. 'And I'm deeply sorry at having to intrude into your privacy, but my proposition... I want you to work alongside me on a certain project I have in mind.'

Ruth thought that she must have misheard what he had said, but, when no further clarification was forthcoming, she said, with a regretful smile, 'I thought I'd made it perfectly clear. I'm hopeless at writing. I don't think I'd be any good at all.'

'You won't be asked to *write* anything. I intend to commence a new series of insights into twenty-first-century life in this so called civilised country of ours by running a selection of interviews with young girls who find themselves lured into teenage prostitution.'

At what point, Ruth wondered, was she supposed to roar with laughter at this outrageous idea of his? Or at least outrageous if he intended to include her in it.

Hadn't she told him that she was a vicar's daughter? She could no more work on such a project than she could strip off all her clothes and streak through a football ground.

'No, I'm very sorry, but I can't...'

'Why not?'

'I'm afraid I'm totally unsuitable for any such assignment,' she amended, smiling. 'Not the right kind of girl at all...'

'Why don't you let me be the judge of that?'

Wasn't he listening to a word she was saying?

'What do you think the *right kind of girl* is?' he asked, walking towards her and then stopping directly in front of her, so that now she had to virtually bend her neck backwards to see his face.

'B-Bold, brassy,' Ruth stammered. 'Self-confident. Perhaps you should ask Jan to do it...'

'That's not the sort of girl I have in mind for this at all,' he said, brutally bulldozing her input without qualm. Then he leaned forward and propped himself up against her chair, gripping either side so that she found herself suffocatingly trapped by him. 'In fact,' he continued softly, his face close enough now so that she could feel his warm breath against her cheek and see the dark flecks streaking the blue irises of his eyes, 'the minute I laid eyes on you I knew that you were the woman I wanted...' He paused, relishing her discomfort. 'For the job.'

At last he stood back, massaging the back of his neck with one hand before taking a more orthodox position on the chair behind the desk.

'My parents...' she protested weakly.

'Would, I'm sure, like to see you spread your wings. It *is* why you came to London, isn't it? Wasn't that what you told me?'

Ruth glared at him, resenting the fact that he had homed in on a passing remark and was now capital-ising on it to justify what he wanted her to do.

'You're a big girl now, Ruth,' he pressed on mer-cilessly. 'Time for you to stop running to Mummy and Daddy whenever you need to make a decision. Time for you to face the big, bad world out there and stop trying to hide away from it.'

'I am *not* trying to hide from anything.' Ruth dug her heels in stubbornly. 'I am just being realistic. My background hasn't prepared me for dealing with a job of that nature...'

'So what do you intend to do with your life? Has it ever occurred to you that the most interesting chal-lenges in life are also often the most threatening?'

He was conscious that what he was trying to do was toe a very delicate line. On the one hand he wanted to coerce her into accepting his offer, into working with him. Partly because he genuinely thought that she would be well suited to what he had in mind; partly because the temptation of being close to her was vir-tually irresistible. On the other hand he was aware that if he pushed too hard she would set her soft mouth in that mute, obstinate line, avert her eyes and simply not budge an inch.

'I'm not going to ask you to do anything dangerous, Ruth,' he said in a gentler voice, resisting the urge to steamroller her into doing what he wanted, even though he knew full well that, underneath the shy ex-terior, this woman was probably immune to being steamrollered. 'I just know that we'll be dealing with young girls, asking them questions of a personal na-ture. They would respond to you far more quickly than they ever would to someone brash and self-assertive. You're gentle and calm enough to draw confidences out of the kind of girls we'll be dealing with, and—who knows?—you might even sway one or two of them to reconsider the road they've chosen.'

Ruth went pink. She couldn't help it. She could feel her soft nature being played on by a master musician, but then he was right. She couldn't run away from everything that had a ring of adventure or risk about it.

He could see the indecision in her eyes and pressed on smoothly, effortlessly, tasting victory. 'Most of our work will be done at night, which is why it's important that you don't have a partner. I wouldn't want to be accused of taking you away from your loved one. You'll be able to work here normally a couple of days a week, but you might find that as your body adjusts to working by night you just want to sleep during the days. And it won't be an assignment that lasts for ever. Two weeks at the most, probably less. Just enough time for us to gain an accurate picture of what's happening to our young people out there and what's being done by the government to put an end to it.'

'Why are *you* so keen to get involved?' she asked, buying time while she mulled over the possibilities in her head. 'Any one of your reporters out there would be more than capable of handling the job.'

'I like to lead from the front.' He shot her a wry smile. 'And maybe you're right about that remark you made to me about being bored.' He shrugged expressively and tried to look humble. 'I have all that I could ever need—or want, for that matter. I started out as a reporter myself, you know.'

He linked his fingers behind his head and leaned back into his hands, staring broodingly up at the ceiling. 'First on a provincial newspaper, ferreting out dirt and scandal, then on a city newspaper as a financial reporter. Good fun and, as it turned out, a useful passport when I decided to branch out and play around with the money markets myself. Since then I've made my money and now—who knows?—maybe I fancy getting back to my roots. Or maybe what I'm looking for is a little...' he leveled his eyes to hers '...excitement.'

Ruth, inexperienced, marvelled at how he could invest a single word with so many hidden, tantalising possibilities.

'Have you told Alison about your idea...for me? I wouldn't want to rub anyone's back up the wrong way...'

'Absolutely,' he said expansively, bringing the palms of his hands to rest on the desk and adopting a businesslike expression. 'Alison thinks it's a fabulous idea, and she's going to rally the other reporters to start working on similar contentious issues so that we can pull something together for the issue due at the end of next month. When you've finished your stint with me, you'll be pulled into a more responsible position—maybe occasionally working alongside one of the reporters as back-up.'

'Oh!' Ruth said breathlessly, a little awed by the suggestion of such a tremendous promotion.

'Naturally, this unexpected change of job will be reflected in your pay.' He whipped a sheet of paper from underneath a paperweight on the desk and waved it in the air, talking at the same time. 'An immediate increase in your salary, to be followed by another increase in three months' time if you prove yourself up to your additional responsibilities—if, indeed, you *want* additional responsibility.

'All you have to do...' he leant across the desk and rapped his finger imperiously at the bottom of the sheet of paper '...is sign here...' He produced a fountain pen, seemingly from thin air, and handed it to her before she could open her mouth to protest at the sudden speed of things.

Ruth's eyes scurried over the closely typed page, briefly taking in the description of her new role, containing an undignified gasp at the enormity of her salary increase.

'At the bottom,' he said. 'Your signature. And then everything's formalised.'

'I'm still not sure...' she said on a deep breath, shifting her eyes away from the piece of paper in front of her with its frightening promises of adventure and money and excitement.

'Of course you are,' he said gently. 'Apprehensive, but sure.'

Ruth frowned, uncertain whether she cared for his ten-second summary of her reaction and then irritated because he was right.

He looked at his watch. 'You're not putting your life on the line with this assignment,' he urged her, raking his long fingers through his hair. 'A week— and if you hate it, believe me, I won't force you to carry on. But give yourself the chance to see whether this kind of thing appeals to you.'

A few more seconds of hesitation and then she put her name at the bottom of the piece of paper. Okay, so she wasn't signing her life away, but the minute she pushed the piece of paper across the desk back to him she felt as though she was signing *something* away, though what she wasn't too sure.

Or maybe it was just that trace of smugness tugging the corners of his mouth that made her feel just a tad nervous about what she had agreed to. She was very nearly tempted to snatch the piece of paper out of his hands, rip it into a thousand pieces and then hustle back to her desk. But, with a speed that left her wondering whether the man was a mind-reader, he folded the paper in half, stuck it into his open briefcase, which was perched on the side of the desk, and decisively slammed it shut.

'Now that's all settled,' he said, standing up and shrugging on his jacket, 'just one or two suggestions before we start work on Wednesday.'

'On Wednesday?' she squeaked.

'Why waste valuable time? No point meeting here. Meet me at The Breakfast Bar in Soho. Here's the address.' He scribbled it down for her and she took the paper from him. 'Eight p.m. sharp. I gather it's where a lot of young girls hang out when they hit London for the first time. It's cheap, in the centre of things, and has a reputation for being a useful place to meet people.'

'How on earth did you find all that out?'

'I'm clever and talented. Hadn't you noticed?' he said in a silky voice, addressing, as it turned out, her downturned head. 'Anyway,' he continued crisply, 'just a couple of suggestions.'

That got her attention. She looked up at him with

her peach-smooth skin and wide grey eyes, now holding a hint of a question in them.

'Dress casually. Jeans, trainers, nothing too...formal. If anything, you'll want to blend in with some of the girls we'll be meeting...that way they'll be more relaxed and more expansive about revealing themselves to a couple of reporters...'

'How do you know they won't laugh in our faces and walk away?'

'I think, actually, they'll either be flattered or relieved that someone's taking an interest in them.' He was by the door now, hand on the doorknob. 'The way we'll play this is: questions in the night, and the following evening we'll debrief over dinner before we start again.' He smiled at her. 'And don't be scared. I'll look after you.'

CHAPTER THREE

'I DON'T know if I'll be able to handle this.'

She had rehearsed a long speech about this, had even stood in front of the bathroom mirror and practised, making sure to keep her eyes focused, to try and control the temptation to eat her words, and to appear confident and firm.

Now, sliding into the seat opposite Franco for the first of their so called debriefing meetings, she found that all of her painstakingly contrived self-assurance had vanished through the window. Her words came out in a rush, and from the expression on his face she could see that he thought she was deranged.

To be greeted by someone whose opening remark was, *I don't know if I can handle this*, must, she conceded, be a little disconcerting.

'Would you like a drink?' was his response, and she looked at him, exasperated.

'No, I would *not* like a drink. I would like to say what I have to say.'

'Go ahead, then.' He sat back in the chair, left ankle resting on right knee, and proceeded to look at her with an interested, patient expression that made her even more nervous.

They had arranged, the night before, to have their debriefing dinner at a pub in Hampstead, which, at six-thirty, was still virtually empty. A few lost souls were perched on bar stools, drinking in a desultory way, and

47

a few more couples occupied tables, but the crowds would not start piling in until later.

Ruth sat very straight on the chair and pressed her hands into her lap. 'I've thought long and hard about this,' she began. 'In fact, I've spent most of the day thinking about it...'

'Are you *sure* you don't want a drink? Dutch courage and all that?'

Ruth hesitated and then nodded briefly. Perhaps a glass of wine. Making her speech had been considerably easier with only her reflection as audience. She watched as he strode off to the counter, leaning against it with his back to her.

He was wearing jeans again. As she had discovered the night before, the attire of jeans, on him, was even more unsettling than a suit, which, rightly or wrongly, exuded more soothing connotations of good behaviour and civilised self-restraint. Seeing him in a pair of jeans for the first time had made her realise that he was younger than she had first thought. He had appeared more overtly sexy in them as he had sat astride his chair, so that the denim tautened and tightened alarmingly over his powerful legs and thighs, chatting easily with two girls who couldn't have been older than seventeen or eighteen.

'So. You were saying?' He handed her the glass, sat back down and proceeded to look at her questioningly over the rim of his glass of lager.

Ruth gulped down some of the wine and then licked her lips thoughtfully. 'I don't think that I handled last night very well,' she began. 'I don't know what I expected when I agreed to this assignment, but the reality of it was just a little too much for me.'

'I thought you were rather good, actually,' he said, massaging the back of his neck with the flat of his hand. 'Concerned, gentle, unthreatening. Kate and Angie seemed to be opening up to you quite a bit.'

'Yes, well, that's the problem. I don't think I want to...' She hesitated, tripping over what was going through her head. 'I'm not gritty enough...'

'Stop right there.' He pressed, palms down, on the circular table and looked at her grimly. 'Now you listen to me, because I'll only say this once. If you don't want to do this, then that's all well and fine, but don't think that you can hide behind a lot of hogwash about *not being gritty enough* and *not being prepared for this kind of thing because you're a vicar's daughter* and *not being the right sort of person.* Just come right out with the truth, which is that this particular assignment doesn't appeal to you. Perhaps you don't like the thought of working nights. Perhaps you just find the girls we'll be interviewing distasteful. Is that it? Have I put my finger on the button? Do you fancy that you're better than they are?'

Ruth's face had turned as white as a sheet, and when she picked up her glass of wine her hand was trembling.

How could he say those things? He had got it all wrong! She had spent hours thinking about what she was going to say, working out her explanations in her head, and when it had come to the crunch her own tongue-tied, gauche, immature stupidity had let her down again! Had left him with all the wrong impressions.

'No!' she protested defensively. 'I have no objection to working nights at all...I don't have any family commitments…and I don't… How can you say that I find those girls…distasteful?' Her voice was shocked and mortified at the assumption, and she watched his expression change from brutal, punishing grimness to something gentler.

'Then what is it?' he asked quietly.

'I…I feel inadequate for the job,' she said finally, which hadn't been part of the rehearsed speech at all. 'I was appalled by those stories last night. Girls who leave home for no better reasons than lack of space and arguments with step-parents—leave home and at the age of seventeen drop the lid on their futures for ever. I wanted to take them home with me and, I don't know…save them, I suppose. Instead I had to jot down every word they said, ask questions and then say good-bye, because tonight we'll move on to a couple of different faces, with different stories and different little tragedies.'

'But you can't make everything better, and hiding away from certain unpleasant realities doesn't mean that they no longer exist. It just means that you remove yourself from the inconvenience of having to confront them.'

Ruth hadn't tied her hair back. Nor had she tied it back the night before. It fell like silk to her shoulders. With her hair loose and wearing a skirt that was a little shorter than normal and a blouse that was a little less buttoned up than customary, she felt strangely vulnerable. She felt like a woman instead of a girl. Particularly here, now, sitting opposite someone so potently masculine and in a situation where the dress code of formality was not in existence.

The night before she had maintained a healthy distance, physically, from him. She had taken up her position on the chair furthest from his, allowing the two young girls to sit between them, facing one another, but, even so, her eyes had slipped towards him with unerring regularity. It was almost as though she had needed to feed off him, feast her eyes on his image, allow his overpowering masculinity to seep into her like a liquid.

She suspected that all this was a little bit puerile, a little bit unhealthy.

Her reaction to him frightened and confused her, and, because she had no slide rule against which to measure it, she ingenuously justified it as perfectly natural, absolutely normal to be fascinated by a member of the species who was so utterly different from any of his kind she had ever met before. She equated it with a lack of logic that she failed to recognise, with the same sort of fascination that might grip her were she to find herself in the company of a two-headed monster.

'I don't have a problem confronting reality,' she said awkwardly.

'Correct me if I'm wrong, but I think that you've led a very sheltered life, very protected, very cocooned. You worked hard at school, did ballet, maybe a bit of horse riding, had every angle of your life mapped out...'

'There's nothing wrong with that!' Ruth burst out vehemently. 'I'm glad I had a sheltered life! I would hate to have been like those girls!'

'Is that why you find it so hard to be in their company? Because you can't identify with them? Because they seem like aliens to you when in fact they're just less fortunate?'

'No,' Ruth said wearily. 'I told you, I just feel too much compassion... I also feel around a hundred next to them, when in fact I'm only a few years older. I feel like their mums and I respond as thought I were...'

'You feel older because of the way you project yourself.'

'What do you mean?'

'I mean...' Here he drew in a long breath and looked at her steadily. 'Look at the way you dress.'

Ruth automatically glanced over herself and blushed.

'You spent the whole of last night huddled in your denim jacket as though you were terrified you might catch something if you took it off.'

'I felt cold.'

'The place was packed with people and it was boiling hot.'

'I...I...' She searched around for a logical reason for her sartorial reticence of the night before and found none.

The truth of the matter was she hadn't dared expose the tiny skin-fitting top she had daringly slung on before she'd left the house. It clung lovingly to every inch of her body. It was the sort of top which was comfortable enough for her to wear at home, when there was no one around, but was absolutely the last thing she would be seen wearing in public. She had no idea why she had worn it. Perhaps she had been imbued with a feeling of recklessness, but, in all events, she had lacked the courage to remove the jacket, even though she had felt stiflingly warm in the café. She was amazed that he had noticed.

'You have the face of a girl, an angelic child, and you dress like someone's matronly aunt, as though you're ashamed of the way you look.' His eyes skirted over her blouse and she nervously responded by fiddling with the top button.

'I'm not a child,' was all she could find to say, hurt by the description.

'You don't have to become these girls' social worker. You simply have to understand what makes them tick—the emotion will transfer itself into what we write, and what we write might change the lives of some of them. There are very good places of sanctuary where they can seek refuge, just until they get their heads together and their lives a bit more sorted out, but, like everything else, these places need government backing. The printed word can work wonders sometimes.'

He could see the awkward embarrassment gradually ebbing away and her eyes lighting up with interest. Woman she might well be, but she responded with the transparently telling emotions of a girl. He could sit and watch the changing expressions on her face for ever. It was as fascinating as watching the rise and fall of the sea on a moonlit night. Her grey eyes reflected the smallest shifts in her moods, from blue-grey, when she felt serene and dreamy, to a stormy dark grey when she was defensive and bristling. Observing all these minute alterations was more fun than reading a good book.

He was also feeling wonderfully fired up. He had watched her covertly the night before, had seen the way her eyes had rested on him before hurriedly flitting away, as though she'd been terrified of being caught out doing something unmentionable. It had been a most amazing turn-on.

She had sat there, her legs discreetly but somehow sinfully clad in what had looked like the thickest possible black tights, her jacket kept severely buttoned so that his mind had been obliged to wander and speculate on what lay beneath it. And when she'd taken notes, which she'd done with remarkable efficiency—he really must see about getting her status at the office changed—her hair had brushed against her cheeks and her fringe, which was short and straight, had become permanently tousled from the way she'd expelled her breath upwards whenever she felt hot or bothered or both.

She was saying something to him, and he shot her a penetrating, earnest look to cover up the fact that his mind had been on a walkabout involving her and her intriguing personality, which seemed to grow more beguilingly addictive with every passing minute.

'Yes,' he said automatically to whatever it was she had said—obviously a question, judging from the way she was looking at him, head tilted to one side, mouth semi-parted so that the smallest sliver of her pearl-white teeth was showing.

'Sorry?' she asked, puzzled.

'What did you say?'

'I asked you what you thought the chances are that those two girls will straighten their lives out.'

'Oh, yes! Right. To be honest, my impression was that they'd done a bunk from Manchester, found themselves in London and were realising that they'd bitten off a bit more than they could chew. I wouldn't be surprised if they started asking themselves whether going back to face irate mums and aggravating siblings mightn't be preferable to the unknown down here.'

'Mmm. I thought that too, actually. In fact...' She rummaged in her bag and extracted her notebook, which she then proceeded to peruse, frowning in concentration. 'Kate pretty much admitted that she was already thinking along those lines. I think it helps that they travelled down together. They prop each other up, whereas they might be more vulnerable if they were on their own, more of an easy target for...undesirable types...you know what I mean....'

'I do,' Franco said gravely. 'Now, what do you want to eat?' He watched her as she glanced around the pub, absent-mindedly pushing her hair behind her ears.

'Anything with chips. I'm starving.'

He fought to conceal a smile. 'Haven't had anything for the day?'

'Not much. Cereal, toast.' She leaned a little forward so that she could decipher what was written on the blackboard on the wall towards the back of the room. 'Fruit and sandwiches for lunch. Nothing since midday, though, which is probably why I'm so hungry.'

He felt a wave of laughter surge through him and he covered his mouth with one hand to stifle the sound. He knew, with unerring instinct, that laughing at her appetite was something she would not find very appealing. He suspected that she might mistakenly assume that he was sneering at her, treating her like a country bumpkin lacking in social graces.

'Are you all right?' she asked, when he was forced

to camouflage his laughter as a choking cough, which made him sound like an old man whose fifty-a-day habit was finally catching up. 'Have you got something in your throat?' She stood up and administered a resounding firm slap to his back, which propelled him forward, mostly through sheer shock.

'What are you doing?' he gasped.

'I thought you might have had something stuck in your throat.'

'What?'

'*I* don't know,' Ruth said, sitting back down and giving him a ladylike glare.

'Must have swallowed the wrong way,' he mumbled. 'Anyway, chips you say?'

'Thank you. With some fish. I see that they do haddock and chips with bread and a salad.'

'Anything else?' He stood up and turned away with an exaggeratedly grim expression, because his lips were beginning to twitch again and another of those slaps administered to his back might cause untold damage to his spine.

Ruth consulted the blackboard again while Franco watched, dumbstruck at the thought that she might actually be considering adding to what she had already ordered, but eventually shook her head in polite denial.

The pub was slowly but surely filling up. Most of the tables were now taken and the only room at the circular bar in the centre was elbow room. Ruth watched as Franco smoothly found a gap and caught the bartender's eye with the practised ease of someone for whom attracting attention was as effortless as drawing breath.

In fact, as she looked at him now, she could see that

the attention he had managed to attract was not limited to the bartender. Women had angled their bodies so that they could surreptitiously snatch a glance or two at the striking man with the pint in one hand, the glass of wine in the other, weaving his way back to the table and... Ruth thought of the image she presented and glumly acknowledged that *the stunningly sexy woman* didn't fit the bill. More likely *fetchingly homely lass.*

'Now,' he said, resuming his seat and pushing the glass of wine over to her. 'What's it to be? Your decision? In or out?'

Ruth gently twirled the glass in a circle on the table, lightly holding it by the thin stem. 'In. But...'

'But...what...?' he asked softly.

'But you put up with me if I occasionally get weepy and sentimental over some of the girls.'

'I'd be surprised if you didn't.'

She wondered whether he would have qualified that as *pleasantly* surprised. 'I'm a weepy, sentimental person at the best of times,' she said, sticking her chin out and daring him to argue the merits of that, which he didn't.

'Don't tell me that you cry at movies?'

'Loudly.'

'And lose sleep over sad stories in the press?'

'To the point of insomnia.'

'And fret if you think you've offended someone?'

'*Ad nauseam.*'

'Then we have a lot in common. I do all those things as well.'

The thought of Franco Leoni sobbing during a movie made her burst out laughing, and she threw her head back and arched into the back of the chair, wiping her eyes. He smiled at her, a long, slow smile, and the laughter dwindled from her lips. The moment of hilarity was gone, replaced by a split second's worth of devastating awareness that seemed to continue into eternity.

Eventually she dragged her eyes away from his face as a harassed waitress appeared with their food, and then the moment was gone, replaced with suitably appropriate chit-chat about their interview the evening before, and how it could be formatted into the report they were building.

Another couple of interviews with youngish girls, he said, perhaps ranging in experience from the newly arrived to the well and truly ensconced. Though those might be less tempted to pour out their hearts and souls because bitterness could be a very effective plug when it came to free speech.

Then they would interview older women, women who had started out down the road years before and ended up at its most logical destination.

'Think you can stand it?' he asked casually, as she tucked into her food, and she nodded without speaking as her mouth was full.

'I shouldn't have any more wine,' she said, when she had swallowed both food and wine.

'Goes to your head?'

'Horribly.'

'And what do you do when that happens?' He leaned forward and his eyes raked over her in a manner that was both casual and searingly intimate. 'Anything that could feed my night-time fantasies?' he murmured in a teasing, playful voice.

'Very funny,' Ruth said severely. She wondered if

he thought she was so thick that she wouldn't recognise that he was making fun of her and her outmoded approach to life, so inconsistent, she knew, with someone her age. 'Now that I've decided...' Was that quite the right phrase? Or would *been persuaded* have been more appropriate? '...to carry on, what shall we do tonight? It's nearly eight-thirty and, well, do we see whether we can do some more interviews? Or not?'

'We do.' He fished in his pocket and withdrew a crumpled-up piece of paper which he proceeded to flatten out. 'I have a couple more contact names and places that we could check out. Nothing quite as salubrious as last night's rendezvous, but then we're looking at girls who are a bit more hardened by life in the big city.'

'Where on earth do you *get* these names and places from?' Ruth asked, peering at the piece of paper.

'Having friends who work in the press can be of great help sometimes.'

He grinned and she said slowly, 'You're really enjoying all this, aren't you?'

'So far.'

'Because it makes a change?'

'Possibly,' he said, with a shrug. He drained the contents of his glass in one long gulp, deposited the glass on the table and said, 'You'll have to change. You're going to stand out in clothes like that where we're going this evening.'

'Where exactly is that?'

'It's the sort of place where good girls don't go. Which is why tonight you're going to have to look like a bad girl so that you can blend in.'

'*Look like a bad girl?*' she asked faintly, her face

registering the impossibility of achieving any such look. 'How does a person *look like a bad girl*? I haven't got that sort of face,' Ruth continued, anxiously contemplating the task and wondering whether this was another well-disguised leg-pulling exercise. 'Would I have to snarl a lot? Bare my teeth? Chew gum? I don't smoke, so that's out.'

'A simple change of outfit should do it. The sort of girls we'll be seeing will be older than the two last night, older, more experienced, and if we want to try and engage their conversation then I suggest you get rid of the buttoned-up shirt and the knee-length skirt.'

'What difference will it make?' Ruth persisted stubbornly. Her skirt, she wanted to point out, was actually a couple of inches above the knee, but he clearly hadn't noticed that.

'It'll be the difference between a possible interview and the possible giving of confidences. A fine but important line if we're to humanise this article we'll be working on.' He stood up and she hurriedly followed suit. 'So. To your place.'

'There's no need for you to come with me,' she said dubiously, eyeing the tall, masculine figure slinging on his battered tan airforce-style bomber jacket and experiencing just the smallest twinge of unease at the prospect of this man being under her roof. 'I can always meet you there…if you give me the address…'

'Absolutely no way. We'll take a taxi to your place. Where do you live?'

It's ridiculous to feel nervous, she lectured herself sternly on the drive over to the flat. It's hardly as though you haven't worked alongside the man now. And anyway, there won't be anything of the social visit about him being in the flat. He'll just be there, waiting while you change. If you change quickly enough you can leave him standing by the front door, even. Maybe. Certainly there won't be any cups of coffee being offered or *Please have a seat; I won't be a minute*.

Why had she thought that he might obligingly remain rooted to the front door while she dashed into the bedroom to change? No sooner had she unlocked the front door and pushed it open than the man was inside the flat, strolling around it with undisguised curiosity, inspecting the books on the single bookshelf over the television set, peering at the family pictures on the mantelpiece by the blocked-up fireplace.

Ruth watched from the open doorway, then she stepped inside and said sarcastically, 'Make yourself at home.'

'This isn't too bad at all, is it?' He made that sound as though his expectations of her place had run along the lines of rat-infested basement studio flat with mould-encrusted lino flooring and peeling paint on the walls.

'What had you expected?' Ruth asked, clicking shut the door and looking at him with her arms folded.

'Nothing as big as this, for a start. Flats in London aren't cheap to rent and I wouldn't have expected that you could afford a decent-sized one-bedroom place.' He looked around him in the manner of an estate agent summing up a potential property. 'With a pretty big kitchen in a respectable area.'

'Actually, Mum and Dad do help me out with the rent,' Ruth admitted.

'Ah.'

Their eyes met and she looked away, nettled by what she felt was going through his head. 'I'll just go and change,' she informed him, scuttling past him towards her bedroom.

She would show him that she wasn't the ineffectual child he seemed to think she was. She glared at her wardrobe, daring it to let her down in her moment of need, desperate to do *something*, project *some* kind of image that would blast a great big gaping hole in his preconceived ideas of her as little Miss Goody-Two-Shoes who thought that a good game of Scrabble was as exciting as sex and who couldn't even make it on her own in the Big Bad World without her parents propping her up on either side.

Useless to explain to him that her parents' financial help was something she accepted because it afforded them peace of mind rather than because she was scared of living somewhere dingier.

Her assortment of clothing was, she was forced to admit, sensible and practical rather than sexy. In the end she made do with a pair of jeans, which she omitted to cinch at the waist with a belt so that they hung low against her slender hips, exposing her belly button. She teamed these with a black and white cropped bra that revealed most of her stomach, over which she flung a cream-coloured cheesecloth shirt which looked the essence of respectability when buttoned up and twinned with one of her pleated skirts, but which reeked of wildness when left hanging open to reveal bare stomach underneath.

She gazed, wonderingly, at her reflection in the mirror and felt a surge of heady abandon.

The girl staring back at her, with the make-up and

the mascara and the figure-hugging, body-exposing clothes, was not Ruth Jacobs. Oh, no. The girl staring back at her was someone wild and sexy and utterly daring.

Well, just for the night anyway.

Ruth grinned at her reflection and stuck her tongue out, then she took a deep breath and went outside.

Franco, staring out of the bay window to the pool of illuminated pavement outside, into which came and went the hurrying figures of people on their way to homes, families, lovers, turned around at the sound of the bedroom door opening.

He'd been thinking how right she was. He *was* having a good time, chasing behind this story with the sort of fervour that reminded him of himself ten years ago, before the acquisition of money had jaded his palate and turned his enthusiasm into dry-tongued cynicism.

And he had to admit that having her along for the ride made things infinitely spicier. Looking at her, enjoying the way she aroused his imagination, succumbing to the novelty of having to take cold showers every night because the slightest passing thought of her turned effortlessly into a network of complex fantasies that would not have gone amiss on the pages of a men's magazine. Yes, he had to admit that his tired soul had been re-ignited in more ways than one.

Even so, it had still surprised him how disproportionately thrown he had been by her suggestion of leaving. He didn't care to question the insanity of his response.

'Well?'

He realised that he had been staring at her. For how

long? He couldn't have said. He knew that his mouth was hanging open, though, and he shut it.

Bad girl. In the low-slung jeans and the small top with enough bare skin peeping through the crack in the unbuttoned blouse to make any red-blooded man need several cold showers on the trot. And, worse than that, there was still enough of the blushingly shy Ruth Jacobs evident to make the picture she presented more hauntingly erotic.

He felt a steady flush creep into his face and he hurriedly cleared his throat.

'Definitely more of a…suitable…suitably appropriate…look. Yes.'

'I haven't overdone it, have I?' Ruth enquired anxiously, peering down at herself, twisting so that she could try and achieve an overall view of herself.

Her fair hair swung over her face and Franco savoured the image she presented of slender, unconscious beauty, moving with the natural grace of youth. Her breasts, he saw, were much bigger than they appeared beneath her normal garb of buttoned-up blouse. The close-cropped top barely provided restraint, and they bounced gently as she inspected herself. He could feel himself begin to perspire and he cleared his throat nosily in an attempt to take control of the situation before he found himself hunting down the nearest shower.

'Not at all. Now, shall we head off?'

Ruth straightened immediately.

His voice was curt, and when she glanced at his face she could see that his expression matched his tone of voice.

Of course she had overdone it. She had been stupidly trying to prove something and now resembled a clown of sorts, right down to the ridiculous clothing and the painted face. As some token gesture to modesty she slung on her denim jacket, so that at least the top half of her body was covered, and then trailed behind him, hovering self-consciously in the background while he summoned a taxi.

She noticed that he barely looked at her for the duration of the drive, which covered a honeycomb of unrecognisable streets and alleys to emerge finally in a long, narrow road which was erratically lit and sported a selection of women lurking in the shadows. Against the walls, in doorways. Singly or else in twos and threes.

Ruth's heart dropped. This was very different from what she had encountered the night before. There was something gritty and depressing and scary about this scene. She drew the jacket a bit tighter around her.

'This'll do,' Franco said, staring impassively out of the window. 'Okay?' he asked in a low voice, when they were out of the taxi, and she gulped and nodded. 'Don't look so terrified.' He walked up to a twosome, who smiled invitingly and told him they were available for some action, whatever he wanted, to which he replied that they were looking for a woman by the name of Mattie.

The process was repeated over and over, until they finally hit jackpot. They were pointed to a building which resembled a warehouse primed for demolition and were told to wait a few minutes because she was with a client.

'How do you know she'll see us?' Ruth whispered, squinting at the black doorway. Ever so often a car would cruise by very slowly. Sometimes there was the sound of doors being opened and closed, then the swish of tyres as the car slipped away. Ruth heard it all like background noise but she couldn't bring herself to look around.

'We don't. In which case we'll just have to try our luck with some of the others. But I think she'll see us. I was given her name by a guy called Robbie, well-known veteran reporter who mostly sits behind the desk now, but years ago he helped her with some police aggro and she's always been grateful to him for that. Now and then they even meet up for a drink. He takes her out for the occasional meal at Christmas time, says that it makes her feel like a worthwhile human being.'

They waited in silence. Ruth had become so accustomed to the slow purr of cars breaking the ominous hush of the dark street that she barely noticed when a car stopped and a man rolled down his window and asked. 'How much, love? When you're through with the next one?'

CHAPTER FOUR

'ARE you *sure* you're all right? Perhaps we ought to go to the doctor…' It was the fourth time in the space of half an hour that Ruth had asked the question, but as she gazed anxiously at the bruised fist resting on his thigh she felt the same mixture of shocked dismay and guilt. 'This is all my fault, isn't it?' she said miserably, thinking aloud rather than posing a question. 'If I hadn't donned this…' she glanced down at herself with scathing disgust '…ridiculous garb, none of this would have happened.' She ran a finger gently along the scraped knuckle and winced on his behalf. 'Is it very awful?'

'Nothing that I can't handle,' Franco informed her stoically. It had taken ten minutes of solid walking and frantic searching before they had managed to find a taxi, during which time he had been pleasantly warmed by her charming show of concern for his welfare.

Whom did it hurt if he had exaggerated a minor scrape into something worryingly more painful?

'I should never have worn this stupid outfit,' Ruth repeated, hunkering down into her jacket as though endeavouring to bury her way through it and vanish completely.

'Will you stop saying that!'

'How can I? I shudder to think what kind of sight I made if that man…that *foul, disgusting, revolting* man thought that I was…available for sale.' She made a choking, disgusted sound under her breath and gazed at her co-passenger in the car with stormy grey eyes. 'I have *never* attracted that *sort of attention* in my life before!' She sounded as horrified as she felt. Her pale blonde hair caught the passing lights and, when it did, shimmered like spun gold. She flicked the spun gold carelessly behind her shoulders and then irritably stuffed it into the back of her jacket.

'You can't be *that* unfamiliar with attention from the opposite sex,' Franco said heavily.

'How much further is it to your house? I did a first aid course when I was at school. I should be able to patch you up in no time at all.'

'Forget the hand,' he answered irritably, not caring for the fact that his usually captivating personality was in competition with a mildly swollen bone on his right hand. 'You haven't answered my question.'

'What question?' She looked up from her frowning inspection of his hand and favoured him with a long, beautifully guileless grey stare.

'I *said*,' Franco repeated, hanging onto his patience, 'you must be quite accustomed to attracting male attention.' He moved his fist from his left thigh to his right, just in case she avoided taking the conversational path he wanted by becoming sidetracked by his now virtually pain-free knuckle. That way, if she was so damned interested in inspecting the offending part of his body, she would have to lean over him which, regretfully, he doubted she would do.

'Well, I haven't got a boyfriend at the moment…' In the darkness of the taxi he could glimpse the faint blush that swept into her cheeks. 'I believe you asked me that question already,' she said, making him feel uncomfortably like a bore.

'Actually, I *wasn't asking you about whether or not you're involved,*' he said, with the bewildering feeling that he had been walking down a straightforward street that had suddenly revealed itself to be a honeycomb of back alleys and side paths. 'I was merely remarking that a girl like you must be accustomed to men staring at her.'

'A girl like me? What kind of girl would *that* be?' Her voice had become frosty with disapproval.

'I'm not implying that you're *any kind of girl* or at least not the kind of girl that you're implying...*I'm* implying...God.' He raked his good hand through his hair. 'You're making me tongue-tied!' He automatically grinned a sexy, rueful grin, but its impact was lost as she was staring fixedly through the car window.

'*Where* did you say you lived? I don't recognise this area at all.' She felt a slight tremor of nerves and wondered whether it had been such a clever idea to offer to help him. He could just have easily have cleaned himself up, but why would he do that when she had rushed in with her exclamations of horror and sympathy and her saint-like insistence that he take her immediately to the nearest first aid kit? Which, he had returned with alacrity, was in the bathroom cabinet of his house.

If she had been thinking with her head and on her feet, instead of with her soft, emotional heart, she would have briskly sent him on his way and headed home to recover from her ordeal.

But guilt had stopped her. She had unwittingly provoked an inappropriate response from a kerb-crawler and Franco had been swift in dealing with the situation. No attempt at an explanation had been made. No sooner had the words left the driver's mouth than he had been yanked unceremoniously from his car, punched even more unceremoniously in his jaw and then flung back into the offending vehicle with a string of abuse, the memory of which was enough to make her go red.

Was it any wonder, she thought now, fighting down her ridiculous surge of nervous tension, that she had felt guilty about the whole thing?

'Chelsea. Just off the King's Road, as a matter of fact. You must have been there since you arrived in London...'

'Oh, yes,' Ruth said vaguely. 'I *did* go shopping there a couple of times, but it was a bit pricey for my liking. The last time my mum came down for a couple of days I took her there, but she spent most of the time telling me that she couldn't imagine *what section of the human population some of those garments in those strange little shops catered for*.'

A look of mischievous amusement crossed Ruth's face. 'She can be a *little* old-fashioned. Poor dear.' She looked with mock gravity at Franco's rapt face. 'She *has* led a rather sheltered life, you know, what with being married to a vicar... Thank goodness she has me to snap her out of it!'

In the silvery light of the car he caught the wicked self-ironic expression on her face and they grinned at one another, momentarily delighted to have found themselves so perfectly attuned on the same wavelength.

Ruth was the first to look away. For some reason

her heart had begun to beat wildly, and maintaining his even, teasingly amused gaze had proved impossible. 'What are *your* parents like?' she asked, licking her lips and struggling not to wilt under eyes that were suddenly strangely disconcerting.

'*Were,*' Franco corrected. 'My father died eight years ago and my mother died three years ago this December.'

'I'm so sorry,' Ruth said impulsively. 'Still, how proud they must have been of you! You've done so much! Built businesses and companies and empires! The lot!'

'Actually,' he said drily, 'my father had done very well for himself on similar lines, so my accumulation of money was not as impressive a feat as it might have been. Not,' he added swiftly, 'that they *weren't* proud of me. Of course they were.

'They were mildly disappointed, though, that I never did the expected thing and married and produced a horde of children. My mother had always longed for a big family, but there were problems and, as it turned out, she was lucky to have had me. But you can imagine the combination of Italian and Irish.' He sighed with heartfelt regret. 'Yes, they would have liked to have seen their only son settled.'

Ruth had a sudden, intriguing image of a settled Franco Leoni, married with lots of miniature Franco Leonis running about. Franco Leoni and babies. Babies and Franco Leoni. Her mouth became dry and her erratic heartbeat did a few flips and carried on at a slightly more accelerated rate.

'Shall I tell you something?' he said, in a faintly

surprised voice. 'I've never come close to telling any-one what I've just told you.'

'Why? Are you ashamed of the fact that your par-ents would have wanted you to settle down and raise a family?' Personally, she couldn't think of anything more pleasurable than settling down with the man you loved and having a family. A nice, large family in a rambling, cosy house where there was always the sound of laughter and music and chatting, where prob-lems were aired and where everyone lent a helping hand to everyone else. She gave a little sigh and half smiled.

'Where are you?' he asked curiously, and she snapped back to the present with a small start.

'I beg your pardon?' she asked, blinking away the pleasant daydream.

'For a minute there I lost you. You just suddenly vanished into a world of your own.'

What he didn't voice was the depth of his frustration as her expression had grown wistful and she had dreamily succumbed to some magical picture in her mind. What he could barely admit to himself was the sharp stab of jealousy as he had sourly surmised that the one thing most likely to put that goofy, happy ex-pression on her face was the thought of some man. Was there someone hovering in the background? Someone perhaps, whom she was not technically *dat-ing* but who still had the power to render her doe-eyed merely at the thought of him?

'Oh, just thinking.' She gave him one of those bland, vague smiles and he frowned at her.

'What about?'

'Nothing in particular.' Her shrug was the physical equivalent to the vague smile and his frown deepened.

'How is it that you never settled down?' Ruth asked, in her soft, direct voice.

With a jolt of awareness he realised that, for all her blushing and ultra-feminine appeal, she was not in the slightest intimidated by him. He was one of the most eligible bachelors in London, if not *the* most eligible, and was respected in every corner of the business community and feared in quite a few. Women flocked around him without encouragement and he had become accustomed to dismissing them with little more than a glance if he so desired. People, he knew, tiptoed around him because of the power and status he wielded. No one, but *no one*, had *ever* asked him why he was still unmarried.

'I mean,' she continued slowly, 'there must be women who find you appealing.'

'Yes, I suppose out there, somewhere, there lurks one or two who don't run screaming from my presence,' he said in an amused, wondering voice.

'I'm sorry. I didn't mean… I just meant that…well, you're…successful, self-employed…and…and…'

'And…?' he encouraged silkily, enjoying this delicious moment, praying that the taxi would linger so as not to spoil it by arriving at their destination with unwanted haste.

'And not ugly,' she said in a rush. 'But really it's absolutely none of my business.'

'Does the classification of *not ugly* count as a compliment?' he asked, with a crooked smile, and Ruth could have groaned aloud in sheer despair.

She had never been the most verbal, gregarious person on the face of the earth, but neither had she ever been quite so stultifyingly gauche as she was in the presence of this man. He had the mysterious power of rendering her almost completely speechless.

'I'm s-sorry...' she stammered. Again. But was thankfully spared a lengthy examination of her clumsy vocabulary by the arrival of the taxi at their destination.

She had expected a house. Out in the country it was a general rule of thumb that the bigger and grander the house and the larger and more impressive the plot of land, the wealthier the inhabitants.

Instead, she found herself peering out at a dubiously large Victorian building which had clearly been sectioned off into apartments. The street itself was divinely quiet, and carried the unmistakable smell of the privacy only vast money could purchase in the heart of London, but she was still surprised at Franco Leoni living in a flat.

'I own a rather grand collection of bricks and mortar out in the wilds of Dorset,' he said into her ear, reading her mind. She heard the smile in his voice and realised that yet again her every passing thought had been displayed on her face.

'How does your hand feel?' she asked, slipping out of the taxi and ignoring the taxi driver's curious examination of her attire in the light of where he was depositing them.

Franco very nearly confessed that he had forgotten all about his so-called injury; then he remembered that the only reason she was here with him now was *because* of his hand. The prospect of her vanishing blithely away in the taxi if he informed her that it felt as right as rain was a possibility he refused to consider.

'Still a bit tender,' he murmured, without a twinge of guilt. He bent over, paid the taxi driver, who was voluble in his gratitude for what had clearly been an over-the-top tip, and then nodded at the block of flats. 'Home sweet home.'

'You mean, *home sweet home, mark one.*'

'Mark three, actually,' he said, extracting a key from his pocket and slotting it neatly into the door. 'I also own another place in Italy.'

'Of course,' Ruth said with gentle sarcasm, turning to look at him fully, 'I'm now beginning to understand how it is that you could buy a company for fun...' She smiled and then turned away to inspect her surroundings.

If, Franco thought wryly, his enthralling personality had taken a back seat to a minuscule bruise on his hand, then it was clear that he had been completely forgotten, lock, stock and barrel, in her absorption with her surroundings.

She audibly gasped as they entered the spacious, heavily modernised hall, which was really presided over by a uniformed porter.

While George, the porter, handed over mail, and pleasantries were exchanged with the comfortable familiarity of two people who see one another daily and go back some way, Ruth stared around her with open-mouthed fascination.

Far from being dark, poky and irremediably Victorian, which had been her expectation, the interior of the grand, renovated house was light and spacious. The cream carpet was thick piled and the paintings on the walls were tasteful and modern. On one wall, stretching all the way up the winding stairwell and breathtaking in its sheer size, was a complex mural that appeared to depict a series of interconnecting mythical creatures. Chandeliers shed a mellow glow and plants were decorously placed here and there so that the overall impression was of space and grandeur.

'Shall we take the lift?' he asked, and she dragged her gaze away from the mural.

'There are *lifts*?'

'Three. One for each of the residents.'

'But surely it won't take long to walk to your flat…?'

'In which case, we follow the winding road until we can't go any further.'

On the way, he explained the mural to her, pointing out some of the well-known mythological figures and most of the more obscure ones. Her child-like enthusiasm invigorated him in a way he would not have dreamt imaginable. He had the empowering feeling that with this chit of a girl at his side he could accomplish anything. How foolish could one grown man get? he wondered.

As they neared the top floor, Ruth felt a sense of apprehension begin to creep over the light-hearted frivolity that had taken them over.

The same plush cream carpet had followed them up the elegant curved staircase, but as soon as he opened the door to his apartment she was confronted with a dose of unbridled masculinity.

Gleaming wooden flooring replaced the thick-piled carpet. As she followed him inside she noticed, in passing, that most of the furniture was solid and exquisitely made but unabashedly modern. Sleek lines, unfettered designs and an absence of anything that was fussy.

'The country house is so full of antiques,' he said, reading her mind again, 'that I decided to go for a totally twentieth-century look. What do you think?'

Ruth paused to glance into the sitting room, where the colours were pale off-whites, creams, with hints of deeper hues in the lush carpets strewn liberally across the floor.

'It's fabulous.' She looked around her and blurted out, a little sheepishly, 'I never knew a Victorian house could look this...this *modern*. The vicarage is Victorian, but...' she smiled fondly at the thought '...absolutely cluttered. Dad's hopeless when it comes to sticking things in drawers, and Mum's almost as bad. This apartment looks as though no one lives in it from one day to the next.'

She gave him a brief, questioning look, and he mildly acknowledged that, once again, his privacy had somehow been infringed.

'I travel a lot,' he found himself saying. 'In fact, as I've mentioned to you previously, I'm out of the country more than I'm in it. And, when I *am* here, I tend to socialise out of the house...'

'Why is that?' She took a few curious steps into the sitting room and looked around her.

'What? Why is what?'

'Why is it that you don't socialise here, when it's obviously huge enough to entertain any number of people? I mean...' She opened her mouth to say something, then promptly shut it again.

'Carry on, carry on,' he told her irritably.

'Nothing. Where have you got your first aid box?' She glanced at her watch, which instantly made him scowl.

'What were you going to say?' he demanded, barring her exit from the room.

'I just wondered whether you never brought anyone back here. There seem to be no feminine touches at all...no flowers in vases or soft cushions...' She looked up at him with interest.

'*Flowers in vases? Soft cushions?* I don't think I've ever dated a woman who was interested in flower-arranging or cushion colour co-ordination.'

'Of course not,' Ruth said quickly, regretting the directness of her question. She could tell from the expression on his face that he was rapidly becoming fed up with her.

'Anyway, I don't care for the thought of some woman spending too much time in my apartment. Naturally I...entertain them here...but I always make it perfectly clear that traipsing in with little jars of female unguents won't do. That's only one short step away from them attempting to make their mark on what they see, which is one even shorter step away from them attempting to do the same to *me*.'

It occurred to Ruth that he had had no problem letting *her* in, listening to *her* remarks about the decor, and was suddenly deflated to realise why. Because he was so uninterested in her as a woman that whether she nosed around his place and proffered her opinion or not was of no concern to him.

'If we could sort your hand out?' she said a little coolly. 'It's late, and I really must be on my way home. I'm whacked.' She yawned in a convincing attempt to provide further evidence of her exhaustion, and in fact, when she had consulted her watch, it was a great deal later than she had imagined.

'In the bathroom,' he said, watching her. He turned away abruptly and headed past a couple more rooms, all equally clinically beautiful as the first, and flung open the door to his bedroom, upon which Ruth halted in her tracks.

'This is your bedroom,' she stated flatly. There could be no mistaking it.

It was dominated by a commanding king-sized bed with an imperious wrought-iron bedhead. The wardrobes were sleekly wooden, and obviously designed and made by the same person who had been responsible for much of the furniture, but there were black iron details picked out in their detail that rendered the final appearance harshly masculine. A tapestry depicting a hunting scene hung over the bed, its rich colours bringing life to the aggressive monochrome scheme. The throw on the bed was black, with ivory lines in abstract patterns, and the pillowcases on the pillows were quite clearly silk, or satin—one black, one ivory-coloured.

It was a room that breathed heavy sensuality. A room that instantly brought on an attack of nerves as Ruth peered around her with alarm.

'Come in, come in,' he commanded, walking towards a door that was old wood halfway up and intricate stained glass for the remainder. 'Don't just stand hovering by the door!'

Ruth cautiously entered the den of iniquity, treading with the delicate hesitancy of someone crossing a minefield. She would get this hand-fixing business over in rapid time and clear out before her nerves got the better of her and induced some horrendously embarrassing Victorian swooning fit.

'Sit on the bed,' he called out, halting her in midstep. 'More comfortable there. I'll bring all the stuff out.'

'It's just a bruise!' Ruth joked weakly to the stained glass. 'No need for that handy vial of anaesthetic!'

He poked his head around the door and shot her a wicked grin. 'I'll just put it back, then, shall I?' He disappeared once more for a few seconds, then emerged with an assortment of things in both hands.

'This is the first aid kit?' Ruth enquired dubiously, shifting back to accommodate the sudden depression in the mattress as he sat down next to her.

She removed her jacket and then examined the sum total of his bathroom cabinet. Some cotton wool, some antiseptic liquid that appeared to have turned a strange, off-putting colour, several assorted plasters, none of which were much good for anything but a minute nick, and, mysteriously, some talcum powder.

'I never said it was comprehensive.'

'Well, it'll have to do.' She took his hand and felt a flutter of awareness as she rested it on her leg, splayed out so that she could examine the bruises, three in all. 'It's really not bad at all, is it?' she mused, head downturned.

For a few seconds Franco was caught between boasting about the fact that the man's face would be looking a damn sight worse than his hand was and assuming the air of a wounded martyr, appealing to the fair maiden for sympathy. He opted for the macho image and said smugly, 'Not bad, considering I probably put the bastard out of action for a few days.'

'You men always think you're so clever, sorting things out with a fight.' She raised her eyes to his and smiled. 'I'm teasing. Actually, you were very gallant. Thank you.' She returned to what she was doing and he felt a wash of unparalleled warmth rush through his body like a tidal wave.

With a mixture of amusement and horror he realised that his body was reacting in its own inimitable fashion, pushing against his trousers, and he shifted his body, crossing his legs awkwardly.

While she worked away on his hand he watched, and gave free rein to a tingling array of erotic fantasies because, with his erection hard and throbbing, thinking chaste thoughts seemed fairly pointless.

'Am I hurting you?' she asked, dabbing the grazed knuckles with the antiseptic ointment.

'No, but you probably could.'

'Sorry?' She looked up and he flushed darkly, quite startled at what had emerged from his mouth.

'What I meant was that you probably *could* hurt me if this ointment wasn't completely ineffective because it's probably been in the cupboard for ten years,' he improvised.

'It *does* look a bit dodgy, doesn't it? Why have you brought talcum powder?'

'Just in case.'

'In case of what?'

'Just in case you wanted to mop things up.'

'Oh. Well, I don't think it'll be necessary.'

'You've missed a bit...there.' He pointed to a scratch that was almost invisible to the naked eye, and as she bent to squint at it, braiding her hair in a make-shift plait to keep it away from her face, he was afforded the sweetest sight he could have imagined possible. The tempting indentation of cleavage, separating the full swell of breasts.

She held his hand between hers, her fingers soft and gentle, and stroked the spot he had pointed out.

'I don't see anything.'

'Are you sure?' His voice was rough and unsteady. Rough and unsteady enough for her to look at him, her hand stilling as she read the flaring attraction in his eyes.

'I think it's time I left,' she said. A similar flush was spreading over her, and her voice sounded wobbly and high pitched.

'Of course,' he said gruffly. 'You need to get to bed.' Neither of them moved a muscle. The silence in the room was now resounding. In her own ears, she seemed to hear the booming of her heart. She had never felt anything as powerful as this. The heat in his eyes scorched her. She felt, literally, as though she was burning up.

'I...I...' she began, unable to rip her gaze away from his.

'You have the most exquisite skin.' He lifted one hand and stroked it. It felt like satin beneath the sensitive pads of his fingers. He watched her pupils dilate, saw the very slight flaring of her nostrils, the fleeting drop of her eyelashes as his finger touched her face, and the impact those physical responses had on him was the equivalent of a powerful electric charge. She tilted her head back a millimetre and her breathing became more ragged.

Looking at her, Franco felt as though he had never before experienced the pull of true passion. It was like being hit, full-on, by a freight train.

Her lips parted, and he leant forward and gently touched her mouth with his, tracing the contours of her pink lips with his tongue, and Ruth gave a moan of desire.

The force of wanting him was so tremendous that she abandoned herself to it. She pulled his head towards her, melting exquisitely as his gentle mouth became hard and hungry and the kiss deepened into a wild, mutual exploration with tongues. She was gasping as his hands found her shoulders and tugged down the lightweight shirt.

Pure sensation seemed to have taken her over, like an alien force, rendering her power to reason completely useless. It was as though her brain had been temporarily switched off at the mains.

She closed her eyes and arched back, supporting herself on her hands. Her legs couldn't be still. They fidgeted of their own accord, lubricated with the feminine moisture oozing like honey from between her thighs.

He leaned to kiss the slim column of her neck and her head fell backwards, her braid coming undone. With his hand, he roughly unravelled what remained tied back and pushed her up the bed, moving with her so that their bodies remained no more than an inch or two apart.

As the palm of his hand pressed between her legs, a firm, moving, rousing pressure through the thick fabric of her denim jeans, she released a long, shaky moan. He undid the button, tugged down the zip and then slid his hand down beneath the tiny underwear, pushing his finger against the pulsating bud of desire and inducing a sharp, sweet feeling of satisfaction.

His finger moved and rotated and she fumbled, eyes still closed, with her tight, cropped top, finally pushing it up and over her breasts in sheer frustration. Her nipples were large and swollen with excitement, and as his finger kept moving against that magical place and his mouth covered the throbbing tips of her breasts, she could no longer contain her mounting need for fulfilment. The thrill of orgasm ripped through her body and she felt herself tense as the waves of pleasure rolled over her.

As she turned to him, appalled at the wanton abandon of her response, wanting only to touch him as he had touched her, the telephone rang.

One loud, shrill summons, followed by another, and another.

'Answer it,' she said, her face stamped with mounting horror as she contemplated what had just taken place between them.

'No way.' He pulled her towards him, but she pushed herself away.

'No!' she cried wildly. She scuttled away from him, rapidly trying to put herself in order and avoid his eyes. 'I shouldn't have... Oh, dear Lord...what have I done?'

'Ruth!'

'Please!' She was almost weeping with shame. 'I'm sorry. Please!'

The phone had stopped and she ran, as fast as she could, past a bewildered George as if the devil was after her.

CHAPTER FIVE

FRANCO had been utterly sure that Ruth would stop working alongside him. The certainty, as he had lain on the bed, cursing himself volubly and aloud for his inept, stupid, thoughtless and downright juvenile handling of this shy woman-child, had twisted in his gut like a blunt knife.

Eight days later and here she was. She hadn't jacked in the assignment, as he had feared, and he could only assume that some little voice in her head had preached to her the values of maturity which would be exemplified if she refused to allow their all too brief moment of exquisite carnal pleasure to come between her and her job.

Now, with their last evening together drawing to a close at a little after midnight, he could feel a disturbing sense of panic that when they parted company now, it would be for good.

He stared at her broodingly, watching how she handled the woman sitting next to her, asking questions without stammering, nodding, murmuring sympathetically now and again, leaning forward to say something so that her hair brushed the sides of her face. She had grown in confidence with every passing day, but far from diminishing her appeal it had added to it.

When the woman finally stood up and took one last long drag on her cigarette, he went through the motions of shaking her hand and thanking her for her time, but he could barely keep the agitation out of his body.

'Do you think we've managed to get enough for the article?' Ruth asked, slipping on her denim jacket.

'I should think so.'

She yawned, and he tried to suppress a childish desire to insist that she give him her full attention. She wasn't even looking at him when she spoke. In fact, she hadn't *looked* at him since the little incident in his apartment. Not once had she mentioned it, but he knew that she hadn't put it to the back of her mind.

The awareness was there all too powerfully in those carefully averted eyes, the surreptitious sidelong glances when she thought he was looking elsewhere, the way she shifted her body away from him whenever he got too close to her, as though she thought that proximity might lead to combustion.

He was experienced enough to recognise all those little give-away signals that told him just how much he still excited her. Unfortunately, he was powerless to do anything about it. His attempts to tease her into relaxing were met with a blank politeness that had driven him crazy.

Now, she was getting ready to go, sticking her little notepad into her bag, checking her jacket pockets, the way she did every night, to make sure that her house keys were tucked away safely in the inner pocket on the inside. In a minute she would get irritated with her hair and shove it into the back of the jacket.

He felt as though he knew her intimately and, worse, still wanted to find out more. Everything, in fact.

Panic was burgeoning into desperation. It was an

emotion so alien to him that he could hardly cope with it.

When had he *ever* been desperate about any woman? His repertoire of emotions when it came to the opposite sex ranged widely from desire to mild curiosity, but certainly never *desperation*.

'Fancy a nightcap?' he asked lightly, slinging on his battered jacket. 'Little celebration to mark the completion of what we set out to do?'

'No, thanks.' She yawned and shoved her hair into the back of the jacket. 'I'm very tired.'

The response, expected though it had been, was still unbelievably maddening.

Begging, he told himself grimly, was an avenue he had no intention of exploring. He could no more beg for a woman than he could swim twice round the world. In fact, swimming twice round the world was probably the easier option.

'What shall I do with all the information we've compiled?' she asked, half turning to him, though still, he noticed, not actually looking at him. 'I could transcribe it onto disk over the weekend. My handwriting is hardly legible!' She pushed open the door of the café and then paused outside for a few seconds, looking around her, getting her bearings.

'Hmm. The information. Good point.' The wind whipped up a bit and he zipped up his jacket, pulling the collar up to warm his face. 'You look as though you're freezing,' he said. 'Have my jacket.'

'No! Don't be silly! I'll be fine once I get into a cab.' She turned and stretched out her hand, which was trembling. 'So it's goodbye, then.'

Ruth smiled at him. The stiff wind had flicked

strands of hair out from the jacket, whipping them across her face so she was forced to gather them up with one hand and then hold them in place.

Thank goodness it was dark. Could he see the tears gathering in the corners of her eyes? Could he see the trembling of her outstretched hand? If he did, she hoped that he would put that down to the cold and not to the dreadful sinking feeling that was pouring through her system like poison.

Of course it was a tremendous relief that they would be parting company. She had tried her very hardest to shove the memory of that humiliating night to the back of her mind, to tell herself that *these things happened*, but it hadn't worked. She had not been able to look him in the face, and it had taken every last ounce of courage to survive the past week and a half.

Once she hopped into the cab and sped away she doubted that she would ever see him again. He hadn't made much of an appearance at the company in the past and he was unlikely to in the future. If anything, her presence there would be enough to ensure his absence.

It hadn't been lost on her that for the past week he had done his best to be kind to her, cracking jokes, teasing her, gamely going along with the pretence that nothing had happened, but she wasn't a fool. He felt sorry for the poor little vicar's daughter who was obviously as well versed in the games adults play as she was in nuclear physics. Which was not at all.

'About all that information...' he said thoughtfully, as they briskly began to cover ground out into the more populated streets, where finding a taxi might pose less of a problem. 'No point transcribing the lot onto disk. For starters, it'll take you for ever.'

'No, it won't. Honestly. I'm quite a good typist.'

'How much have you actually got?'

'Quite a bit, as a matter of fact,' she admitted, panting as she tried to keep up with his much longer strides. 'I had no idea how much note-taking I'd done until a couple of days ago when I gathered it all together.'

'As I thought,' he said, trying to keep a note of crowing triumph out of his voice. 'Reams of information. Far easier if I sift through it first and highlight the important areas. *Then* you can transcribe it to take in to work.'

'Okay,' she said easily. 'Shall I get a courier to take it to your office on Monday?'

He appeared to give this a bit of thought. ''No,' he finally said, drawing out the single syllable so that it reverberated with sincere regret that he couldn't be more accommodating. 'Don't forget, time is of the essence if we're to get this out for the next issue, or at the very least the issue after. I'll come over to your place tomorrow evening, let's say around seven? Seven-thirty?' He had spotted a taxi and was flagging it down.

'My place?' Ruth gulped, and with the best will in the world couldn't keep the tremor of trepidation out of her voice.

'Don't put yourself out by cooking anything elaborate. Just something simple, or I could bring a takeaway…' He had pulled open the door to the taxi and was shovelling her inside. 'I'll get another taxi,' he informed her, leaning into the cab. 'So, that's settled, then, is it? Your place tomorrow. Takeaway? Or will you rustle something up?'

'Well…' she began desperately. Visions of any such scenario transpiring had not occurred to her. Consequently, she had no weapons at hand with which to deal with it.

'Honestly, Ruth, pasta will be great.' Before she could frame an answer to that self-imposed invitation, he had turned away and was rattling her address to the taxi driver, then he gave her a brief salute, nodded, and said, 'See you tomorrow, then.'

'Yes, but…' Her words were lost in the heavy slam of the door and then the taxi was pulling away from the kerb and Franco, as she looked back, was a rapidly diminishing figure, before disappearing altogether as the car rounded a corner.

She was dimly aware of having been railroaded into something, but then decided that she was being fanciful. What incentive did Franco Leoni have to railroad her into anything? His primary concern was for the magazine, and he was right. They couldn't afford to sit around, and if he sifted through all her transcripts tomorrow then she would have all of Sunday to type up the relevant information.

So why, she wondered, did she spend the whole of Saturday feverishly buying food and tidying her little flat and generally acting as though his casual visit, arranged out of necessity rather than choice, was *a date*?

His suggestion of a simple pasta meal had been the starting point for one of her specialities, a prawn and tomato dish, lathered in a rich, creamy sauce, which was excellent with penne pasta and asparagus. Going strictly in accordance with her own appetite, she made sufficient to feed a small army.

It was only when the cooking had been accomplished, and she stood back to survey her handiwork, that a sudden, unappealing thought occurred to her.

Franco had mentioned, in passing—she couldn't remember exactly *when*—that he disliked women fussing around him. She wondered, with a groan of despair, whether he might read all the wrong things into what for her had been doing something she basically enjoyed. Would he imagine that she was trying to impress him with her culinary skills? Ingratiate herself under his skin?

Once the notion had taken root, it grew with remarkable speed. By the time six-thirty had rolled around, Ruth's imagination had leapt ahead to a scenario that involved Franco inspecting her lavish offerings with contempt and then leaving as quickly as his feet could take him, forgetting all about her transcripts in the process, and having to bellow up to her to fling them down.

To compensate for the meal, she opted for the least attractive clothing in her wardrobe. A pair of green chinos that were a size too big for her and consequently made her look ridiculously thin and unfeminine and an off-white shirt that had belonged to her father before she had decided to appropriate it for her own use years previously.

The shirt hid everything and the trousers made her look like a boy. In fact, the whole get-up was eminently satisfactory, given that she wanted to imply to her uninvited guest that his presence was something she could take or leave, that she had certainly gone to no trouble on his behalf, and that the abundance of food was more to do with her own hearty appetite than it was to do with impressing him.

By the time the doorbell rang at precisely seven-fifteen, Ruth had collated every single piece of paper-work and had stacked it with mathematical precision in the middle of the coffee table in her tiny sitting room. Even someone with appalling vision would not have missed the telling bundle.

'For you,' were his opening words.

He was dressed as casually as she was, though his uniform of jeans, which he had adopted for their nightly meetings, had been replaced by dark grey cotton trousers and a grey and black striped polo shirt, just visible beneath his jacket.

'You shouldn't have,' Ruth said automatically, taking the bottle of wine from him and thinking, dubiously, that she was less than grateful for the gesture, though she knew that it stemmed from nothing more than politeness.

''Course I should. I've disturbed your weekend. Made you rearrange your plans, most probably.' He paused, and then added casually, 'Have I? I hope not.'

'Oh, nothing that I can't arrange for another evening,' she answered vaguely, stepping aside to let him enter and then shutting the door behind him.

Her cagey reply, Franco thought with a twinge of irritation, was not exactly an auspicious start to the evening, but he would overlook it, skirt round the temptation to pry further, until he elicited a response that was more to his satisfaction. It was just ridiculously good to see her again.

'Smells good in here.' He sniffed the air appreciatively while divesting himself of his jacket. 'You haven't put yourself to any trouble, have you?'

'No more than I would have for anyone coming over for a meal, even if it *is* a working meal.' She took his jacket, placed it on the hook on the wall by the front door and headed towards the bundle of paperwork.

'Aren't you going to offer me a drink?' He reached for the bottle of wine. 'Point me in the direction of a corkscrew and I'll pour us both a glass.' He didn't wait for an answer. Instead, he spun round on his heels, and she hurried in front of him before he could get to the kitchen and start making himself at home, rooting through her drawers in search of a corkscrew, peering into her cupboards in his hunt for two wine glasses.

'Give it to me,' she said breathlessly. 'You can wait in the sitting room. In fact, you could start having a look at my notes.' If she lingered in the kitchen long enough he should have ample time to flick through what she had written, which would speed the evening up no end.

He seemed to have taken over her small flat with his presence and her hands were shaking as she tried to manipulate the wretched corkscrew. Eventually she managed to pop the cork out and she tipped a generous glassful into two water goblets, which were all that she possessed that remotely resembled wine glasses. Similar shape, loosely speaking, although, she noted wryly, they held considerably more. She would have to take her time with hers or her brain would be further addled.

She returned to the sitting room to find him poring

over sheets of paper. Very businesslike, very promising, very *not* a social visit.

'Ah, glad you came.' He patted a space next to him on the sofa just as she was about to hand him his glass and retreat to the furthest corner of the room. 'You were right about your handwriting. Very difficult to read. I'm afraid you're going to have to decipher some of these squiggles for me.'

Caught on the hop, Ruth hovered uncertainly for a few seconds, then she handed him the wine glass. He beamed encouragingly at her and patted the vacant space a little more firmly.

'What, for instance, does *this* say? It looks as though something small and eight-legged decided to go for a walk across the page.'

Ruth scuttled around the table and perched next to him, peering at the paper.

'Oh, that's a word-for-word account of the conversation we had with Amanda? Do you remember Amanda?'

'Short spiky hair?' Bad complexion? Fidgeted a lot?'

'Yes, that one.' She rattled off what was on the page, bending slightly across him.

'And what about this?' He jabbed another page, just as she was about to pull away.

'Here, hand me the paper,' Ruth told him, suddenly aware of his clean, crisp masculine smell and the fact that her arm had been only an inch or so away from his thigh. She pulled it out of his hand towards her and he edged closer until their bodies were touching very lightly, then he bent a bit, his left hand sliding over the back of the chair behind her head.

He had a hot vision of her nakedness, the way her fiery body responded to his touch, every inch the passionate woman underneath the gauche, sweetly shy, dreamy girl.

He tried to focus his eyes on the piece of paper in front of him, knowing that he had to keep her talking just to be near her like this. He crossed his legs and attempted to shove the insidiously erotic images out of his head. The sight of his erection pushing against his trousers would be enough to send her running out into the street in a state of terror, most probably.

'Sorry?'

'I said that I'll write the indecipherable bits a bit more legibly in the space above.' She tilted her face to his and narrowed her eyes. 'Are you listening to me?' She became aware of his arm extended behind her and abruptly stood up. 'I'll go and see about the food. If you could just highlight the bits you don't understand in one colour and highlight the bits you want transcribed in another, then we should be able to go from there.'

'What about the bits I can't understand but *might want transcribed*? Use both colours? Or do we bring in colour number three?'

Ruth gave him a stern, reproachful stare. 'Now you're just being silly.'

'Sorry,' he said meekly. 'Saturday night levity.'

'I'll be in the kitchen.' She spun round on her heels and was busily setting the small pine table and heating the food when she became aware that he was in the kitchen with her.

'Have you finished already?' she asked, turning

round to face him, her face flushed from the heat, and drying her hands on the striped apron she had slung over her clothes. She had scraped her hair away from her face into a high ponytail. It swung gently behind her every time she moved her head.

'You *have* put yourself out,' he said, beelining to the saucepan and the pots simmering gently on the stove.

'No, I haven't!'

'There's enough food here to…'

'Go away. You're…you're disturbing my concentration!'

'Oh, really?'

She felt his attention on her as she turned away and realised that her words could easily be misconstrued.

'I mean,' she said, very quickly, 'I hate people being in the kitchen when I'm cooking, peering at the food and…' she looked at his hand '…sticking fingers in to taste.'

The hand was immediately withdrawn and he threw her a sheepish little-boy look which just made him look even more alarmingly sexy.

'I'll just sit at the table,' he told her. 'You won't notice that I'm here. You just carry on. I'll be as quiet as a mouse.'

'What about the work?' she asked, watching in dismay as he settled comfortably into one of the four small pine chairs.

'Work can wait a while. I have a feeling it won't take as long as I thought.' He gave her a charming grin. 'I take it you enjoy cooking?'

Ruth stirred the pasta and then fetched the salad out of the fridge and stuck it on the table in front of him.

An Important Message from the Editors

Dear Reader,

Because you've chosen to read one of our fine romance novels, we'd like to say "thank you!" And, as a _special_ way to thank you, we've selected _two more_ of the books you love so well, _plus_ an exciting mystery gift, to send you absolutely FREE!

Please enjoy them with our compliments...

Rebecca Pearson

Editor

P.S. And because we _value_ _our customers, we've attached something extra inside..._

Peel off seal and Place inside...

How to validate your
Editor's FREE GIFT "Thank You"

1. Peel off gift seal from front cover. Place it in space provided at right. This automatically entitles you to receive 2 FREE BOOKS and a fabulous mystery gift.

2. Send back this card and you'll get 2 brand-new Harlequin Presents® novels. These books have a cover price of $3.99 each in the U.S. and $4.50 each in Canada, but they are yours to keep absolutely free.

3. There's no catch. You're under no obligation to buy anything. We charge nothing—ZERO—for your first shipment. And you don't have to make any minimum number of purchases—not even one!

4. The fact is, thousands of readers enjoy receiving their books by mail from the Harlequin Reader Service®. They enjoy the convenience of home delivery...they like getting the best new novels at discount prices BEFORE they're available in stores...and they love their *Heart to Heart* subscriber newsletter featuring author news, horoscopes, recipes, book reviews and much more!

5. We hope that after receiving your free books you'll want to remain a subscriber. But the choice is yours— to continue or cancel, any time at all! So why not take us up on our invitation, with no risk of any kind. You'll be glad you did!

6. Don't forget to detach your FREE BOOKMARK. And remember...just for validating your Editor's Free Gift Offer, we'll send you THREE gifts, *ABSOLUTELY FREE!*

GET A FREE MYSTERY GIFT...

YOURS FREE!

SURPRISE MYSTERY GIFT COULD BE YOURS _FREE_ AS A SPECIAL "THANK YOU" FROM THE EDITORS OF HARLEQUIN

Visit us online at
www.eHarlequin.com

'Yes, I do.' Her voice softened. 'Mum and I used to spend every Sunday in the kitchen when I was a girl. She'd let me roll pastry for pies and knead dough for bread, and when I got a little older I'd chop and mix and stir. I've always associated cooking with fun.' He had brought her glass of wine into the kitchen and she absent-mindedly picked it up from the kitchen table and swallowed a mouthful.

Then she drained the pasta and stirred in some black pepper and parmesan cheese. She brought it to the table with the pasta scoop stuck in, then the prawns, thick and creamy and a rich tomato-red.

'Just help yourself,' she instructed. She divested herself of the apron, slung it back over the hook, and didn't demur when he topped up her glass with some more of the crisp white wine.

'Now sit down,' he commanded, when she continued to hover as he helped himself to food.

Ruth sat down, politely waited until he had finished, and then helped herself to her usual giant-sized portion of food. When she looked up, Franco was staring at her plate with wonderment.

'I enjoy eating,' she said defensively, and his mouth curved into a slow, long smile.

A man could grow ridiculously accustomed to her honesty, he thought. All of a sudden, memories of drawn-out games he had played with the sophisticated women he had always tended to date seemed trite and pointless. Why didn't *all* women say what was in their heads, instead of batting their eyelashes and flirting and never calling a spade a spade?

Meals for the rake-thin glamour models of his experience were lettuce leaves and carrot shavings and fat-free vinaigrette. Anything more substantial was tentatively nibbled and then fashionably left. Conversation never expressed real thoughts or opinions or feelings. Conversation, he realised, was always merely a prelude to sex.

'Do you know,' he murmured, following her lead and devouring his food with the zeal of someone unexpectedly rescued from starvation, 'that the enjoyment of food is often linked to a sensual nature?'

'Sorry?' She paused in mid-mouthful to look at him.

There was a dab of sauce in the corner of her mouth and she licked it away with a gentle flick of her pink tongue, like a kitten. Franco wondered how it was that there wasn't a barrage of men beating down her door. Was it only him who found her the most erotic woman on the face of the earth? He shovelled a mouthful of pasta and prawn into his mouth.

'I *said* that appreciation of food is often linked to an appreciation of all things…physical.'

The gist of what he was saying crawled into her head, delightfully fuddled by the single glass of wine she had consumed, and a slow spark of excitement began to burn.

He stuck his fork into his salad and looked at her. 'You are a very sensual woman, Ruth.'

Ruth stared at him, shocked at the unexpected directness of his remark. She carefully returned her wine glass to the table and took a deep, steadying breath.

'I don't think this conversation is…is… appropriate,' she said in a whisper, clearing her throat.

'I'm paying you a compliment, not launching into a debate.'

'Yes, well, that's as may be...'

'But...? Are you so unused to being complimented by men that you're incapable of accepting one? In the manner in which it was intended? Or maybe you find it uncomfortable to think of yourself as a woman who might enjoy sex...'

The fork, which she had been holding, clattered to her plate, and she hastily retrieved it and licked it clean. Her eyes skittered from plate to glass and back to plate, frantically trying to avoid resting on his face.

'Were your parents inhibited when it came to the question of sex?' he pressed on, watching as her face went from pink to white and back to pink. 'Was it something that was never mentioned at home? Are you ashamed of your body? Of how it feels when you're turned on?'

'No! No, no, no!' She stood up, her hands pressed over her ears, her eyes shut.

Why was he doing this? Why was he pushing her to the limit? What did he want her to say? That, yes, she liked being touched? That he turned her on? That she couldn't lay eyes on him without every pore in her body going into hypersensitive overdrive?

She felt his hands on hers and he gently pulled them away from her ears.

'I can't go on pretending that nothing happened between us, Ruth,' he said softly. 'Even though I know that's what you want more than anything else...isn't it?'

'I don't see the point of discussing it,' she whispered miserably.

'But it won't go away, will it?' He tilted her face up to his and smiled crookedly at her. 'The last week has been agony. Looking at you, wanting you, knowing that you want me as well. Because you do, don't you…?'

'No!' Ruth cried wildly, struggling against hands that were gripping her like bands of steel. He waited until her futile struggles had petered out.

'So if I kiss you,' he murmured, his voice deepening, 'you won't respond…?'

She looked at him then, her eyes wide with dismay.

'I…I…' The balance of what she had intended to say was lost as his lips found hers, then it was as if a dam that had been feebly contained had suddenly and irrevocably broken its barriers.

She was clutching him, gripping his arms and returning his kiss with fierce, hungry craving. She could taste sauce and wine on his tongue and she sucked it compulsively, enjoying his fast, uncontrolled breathing and the way his hands, behind her head, curled into her hair, dragging it free of its ponytail.

He scooped her off her feet and into the bedroom and she watched, feverishly, as he stripped off his clothes. Oh, his body! Lean, hard, every muscle toned and rippling as he yanked off the shirt and then his trousers, flinging them to the ground impatiently.

His erection was hard and big and he smiled as her eyes fastened on it.

'This is what you do for me,' he said thickly, touching himself, and she moaned softly under her breath. Instinctively she began undoing the buttons of the shirt, frantically tugging at them while he watched, enjoying every deliciously sweet moment of what was happening between them, of what was to come.

Anticipation had never before been filled with such agonising, piercing ecstasy.

She heaved a sigh of relief as he unclasped her bra and tossed it to the ground, where it joined the discarded shirt. His sharp intake of breath as he looked at her naked breasts hitched her levels of excitement yet higher. Considering her build was slight, her breasts, she knew, were full, with large nipples now pointing upwards, as though beckoning his mouth. She touched one with the tip of a moistened finger and his throbbing member stirred in heady arousal.

Her trousers felt heavy and cumbersome against her legs and she ripped them off with shaking hands, watching him all the time. Watching him, watching her.

Restraining himself was excruciating, but Franco had learnt from his one experience with her. He wanted everything to go slowly now. No fast foreplay and urgent, solitary orgasm. He wanted to touch everywhere, with every part of his body.

He waited until all her clothes were off and she was lying in naked splendour on the bed, her hair falling against the pillow in a pale sheet, her slender body hovering on the boyish were it not for the full, ripe swell of her breasts. Then he moved slowly towards the bed and over her, his body skimming hers but not resting on it.

Very delicately he explored her mouth and lips with his tongue, and when she tried to press him harder against her he laughed softly and stroked her hair.

'Oh, no, you don't. This time I want us to enjoy one another.'

So she steadied herself, and gradually her body

melted under the slow, erotic, lingering caresses. One touch and her whole body tingled. Her breasts she offered to his mouth like ripe fruit and watched his dark head as he suckled on them, slowly taking his time, moving down her stomach and finally finding the honey sweetness he craved.

He nuzzled and burrowed into the shell-like pink lobes that hid her quivering womanhood, enjoying the thrusting of her hips which she couldn't control as the waves of pleasure rippling through her grew more intense.

Her body, under his touch, was like a magical instrument, and he felt both privileged and humbled by her granting him permission to play.

And he seemed tuned in to her in a way he had never felt with a woman before. When he knew that the urgency of her movements would soon spill over into unstoppable pleasure he moved over her, kissing her neck, her lips, her eyes, wanting to kiss every bit of her, missing nothing out.

'Oh, my darling.' His voice didn't sound as though it belonged to him. It was husky and unsteady and unrecognisable.

Her eyes flickered open.

'What is it?' he asked, stilling.

'I've never…you know, I…I'm a virgin.'

'I'll be gentle.' Was he in heaven? He closed his eyes and breathed her in deeply.

Oh, his love, and for his eyes only.

CHAPTER SIX

QUICK learner had never been a description applied to Ruth. At school, she had got there in the end, but she had never been one of those bright young things whose hands had always been raised to tell the answer, who had achieved B grades without benefit of revision, who had been able to spend their time giggling with the boys at the back and yet, mysteriously, had still known the answers to the maths questions when asked.

Ruth had plodded. *Tries hard* had always been somewhere in her end of term report cards.

Now, in the space of four weeks, she had proved a very quick learner indeed. She had returned to her normal duties at the office and had known, without having to be told, that what was going on between her and Franco was not for public consumption.

She had caught on in double-quick time that, although she had lost her footing and was falling inexorably in love with him, the feeling was not mutual. *Love* was a word that had not once crossed his lips, and she took great pains to hide the way she felt because she knew that if he discovered the truth he would politely turn away, and she preferred the agony of her pointless love to the certainty of his absence.

So at work she smiled, and was as obligingly in the background as usual, happy to run her errands and pleased that she was being given more responsibility.

There was some mention of her going on a short writing course, so that she could help out on some of the more straightforward feature articles, which would be exciting, and when that happened she would be released from some of her more mundane duties.

She had never been one for talking about her private life, which she had always considered deeply boring anyway. People had become accustomed to her shy reticence on the subject. No one suspected that now, beneath that quiet, smiling reserve, was a new and thrilling love-life. No one would have guessed in a million years that three or four times a week now, when she left the office, it was to rendezvous with Franco, whose company, against her better judgement, became more addictive by the day.

He never failed to delight her. She could listen to him chat for hours, although that never happened because he always insisted on hearing what *she* had to say. He always seemed to find her anecdotes amusing. He could be so tender and yet so hungry, taking her with a passion that left her breathless.

The only thorn in her paradise was the fact that their relationship had been doomed from its inception. One day, sooner rather than later, the hot desire that simmered in his eyes every time he looked at her would fade away into bored uninterest. His amusement at her gauche little ways, which she could no more help than she could prevent the sun from rising in the sky, would turn to indifference. He would cease to complain at the times they could not spend together and instead begin to find ways of lengthening the absences between them.

She found herself swaying on the underground train one morning, lost in her reverie of doom and gloom.

It couldn't get any worse, could it?

The thought, which had been creeping under her skin, burrowed deep in her subconscious like a malignant germ waiting for the right moment to emerge, began to gently flower amongst the rich soil of her depressing thoughts.

A wash of hot blood flowed upwards to her face and she could feel a fine perspiration break out over her body.

By the time she arrived at her stop, five minutes later, her limbs were numb. Of course she was worrying needlessly. Hadn't that always been one of her traits? Hadn't her parents always fondly told her that she was a little worry-wart?

But where *was* her period? She didn't keep a rigid check on them, although she usually more or less knew when they were due, but she was uneasily aware that she was late. *How* late she couldn't say for sure, and she clung to this thought as her feet swerved away from her normal route to work to detour into the chemist's on the corner.

I can't be pregnant, she thought, sick with panic. *We've been so careful.*

But there had been that one time, hadn't there? The first time they had slept together had been unprotected, hadn't it?

Her mind continued to conduct a two-way debate on the subject even while her hands reached for the pregnancy testing kit and her eyes read the brief directions on the outside. She weakly struggled to convince the treacherous inner voice in her head that she was being silly while she paid for the kit, and her feet somehow found their way out and began walking to work.

One minute. It took one minute for her world to fall to pieces. In the small confines of the office toilet, ears attuned to the slightest sound of anyone coming in, the give-away box and its wrappings scrunched up into a small bundle and shoved into the disposal unit next to the toilet, Ruth watched in horror as one thin blue line was joined by another above it.

'Oh, no!' She realised that she had groaned aloud, and she clasped her hand to her mouth, biting back the cry that wanted to come out. 'I can't be.' She picked up the plastic gadget and stared at the message it was flamboyantly telling her. Her hands were shaking violently and she sat down on the lid of the toilet and tried to order her thoughts.

Eventually she shoved the tube into the disposal unit, washed her face with ice-cold water and looked at her reflection.

A baby. You're going to have a baby. You're pregnant!

Who would ever have convinced her that the one event which she had spent her life looking forward to would induce feelings of horror, shock and sick despair?

She was hanging onto either side of the sink, fighting down the nausea clambering up her gullet like acid, when the door was flung open and Alison strode in, bursting with vitality and in the middle of some particularly pleasing thought that had brought a smile to her lips. She stopped dead in her tracks when she saw Ruth, now hurriedly trying to look normal, inclined over the sink.

'What the heck…? What's the matter, Ruthie?'

Ruth gave her a watery smile and desperately racked her brains for something to say. 'Nothing. I just…it's not a good morning for me,' she finished lamely, and truthfully.

'What's wrong? What's the matter?'

The door was pushed open and Alison flew to it and snapped at the hapless intruder to leave, then she turned to Ruth.

'Has something happened? What? You'd better sit down. You look as though you'll fall down otherwise.' She guided Ruth to the chair in the corner and sat her down, invalid-style, then she squatted next to her and held her hands. 'Has something happened to one of your parents?' she asked anxiously. 'Is someone ill?'

An idea stirred in Ruth's head and she took a deep breath. 'It's my mum. She's not very well at the moment.' It wasn't, technically speaking, a lie. When she had last spoken to her mother two days previously her mother had been complaining of a cold, some nasty little virus that was flying round the village and taking its toll.

'Oh, Ruth.' Alison's eyes brimmed over with sympathy and Ruth felt a twinge of unpleasant guilt, but what else could she do?

In the space of three seconds, as soon as she had discovered that she was pregnant, she had known two things very clearly. The first was that she was not going to get rid of the baby and the second was that she would have to leave her job, leave London, and leave

Franco for good. The baby would be *her* responsibility and hers alone.

Now Alison, unwittingly, had provided her with a way out. At least a way out of the job, and, much as it sickened her to play on her boss's softer nature, she could see no way around it.

'Shall we go into my office and discuss it?'

Coffees were brought in, and the force of curiosity pressing against the closed office door was almost enough to break it down.

Ruth hatched her plan, through necessity and desperation. She would take a few weeks off, at her insistence unpaid, keeping in contact with the office by phone.

'We've got your address on file, so we can contact you if needs be, can't we?'

The only address on her work file, Ruth knew, was her London address, and she planned on being out of the city before the week was finished. No one knew the whereabouts of her parents. She tried to remember if she had mentioned it to Franco at any point, but she was sure that she hadn't.

He knew that she had grown up in a village and that her father was a vicar, but that could apply to millions of villages in the country, so if he tried to look for her he would bump into dead ends, and she doubted that she was an important enough fixture in his life for him to pursue it too assiduously.

'Are you sure there's nothing more we can do to help? I'm sure Franco would—'

'No! Please,' Ruth interrupted quickly. 'Honestly, Alison, he's done enough for me already, what with this promotion and stuff. I'm only sorry that I won't be able to take advantage of it.'

'You will when you return.'

'Yes, that's true.' She looked down briefly at her hands and her eyes fell onto her flat stomach. In a few months' time she would be feeling the movements of this baby inside her. Her job at the office was over, thanks to one night of stupidity. 'It's been brilliant working with you. With all of you.' Her voice trembled and the worry returned to Alison's face.

'Why are you talking as though we're losing you for good, Ruth?'

'Well, you can never tell...'

'Don't be so pessimistic. Your mum'll be fine. My mum fell and broke her hip a year ago, and we all thought that she would be out of action for good. But two months later she was back on the golf course, hale and hearty as a horse and chivvying the lot of us around, as per usual.'

'Yes, well...' If only it were as simple as that. She hadn't even gone down the road of contemplating how her parents would react to her news. She would have to brace herself for that, but she knew that it would break their hearts. She felt her eyes begin to sting and she blinked rapidly, and shoved the thought to the back of her head.

By the time the day was done Ruth had returned to her flat, drained. At least there would be no Franco to face. He was out of the country for the next week and, although he would call, she could easily cope with his voice down the end of a line. Alternatively, she could always fail to pick up the telephone and let the answer-machine take a message. Cowardly, but so much easier than dealing with him verbally.

Everything moved so quickly after that, that Ruth barely had time to pause for breath.

Two phone calls to the office, to inform them that she would keep in touch, and Franco's calls she steadfastly ignored. Though she listened to them as they were recorded on the answer-machine, her stomach clenching into knots as, over the week, his tone of voice became progressively angrier at her absence. If she hadn't known him for the man that he was, allergic to all forms of commitment, she might well have imagined that there was a possessiveness to his voice that she had never noticed before.

A gullible fool might well have read all sorts of things into that, but time had hardened her. Before, she had been able to put up with him because she loved him, and because she had been prepared to face the inevitable hurt when he grew weary of her. The baby changed everything. Several options presented themselves if she stayed to tell him the glad tidings.

The first was that he would be furious. He might even see it as some kind of elaborate trap to force him to settle down, and she would have to watch any fondness he might have had for her curdle into contempt and dislike.

The second possibility was that he might actually force her to marry him, and thereafter she would have to endure a life chained to his side, helplessly in love, while he did his duty as a father and fulfilled his needs as a man elsewhere. Because there could be nothing more conducive to rotting a relationship than a shotgun wedding.

The worst scenario involved him fighting her for custody of the baby, and, naïve though she was, she was not so naïve that she didn't know that money spoke volumes. He had lots and she had none.

Whichever way she looked at it, running back home was the only solution she could see to her dilemma.

On the Friday morning she stood at the door of the flat which had once brimmed over with all her hopes and dreams and excitement, and looked at the impersonal space staring at her. She had packed all her clothes into two large suitcases. The rest she had crammed into the small van which she had rented for the trip back home.

It had taken under three hours, but in that time she had felt as though she was packing away her youth. When she arrived at the vicarage it would be gone and she would begin a new life altogether. One where love was only a memory and the past was something to be unlocked at night and treasured.

At least, she thought, as she cautiously began the long drive back home, she had concocted something to tell her parents. It was a lie, and a fairly horrendous one at that, but Ruth steadfastly told herself that it would be a lie in a good cause. There was no way that she would be responsible for breaking her parents' hearts.

It would be bad enough when they discovered that she was pregnant, but they would be devastated if she told them the circumstances behind the pregnancy. Out of wedlock, deeply in love with a man who did not return her love. The unspoken postscript to that would be the tacit admission that he didn't love their daughter but he was willing to use her for sex and, worse, she had allowed him.

Sex, the most beautiful demonstration of love between a man and a woman, degenerated into an animal act to satiate lust. They would never dream of castigating her, but it would be in their eyes for the rest of their days and Ruth just couldn't face a lifetime of silent reproach.

So as the van neared the vicarage she plastered a joyful smile on her face as her mother ran out to greet her. They were expecting her. There would be an enormous welcoming lunch, probably her favourite of fried fish and homemade chips with lots of bread and butter and mushy peas. They would sit down with anticipation glowing on their faces to hear this incredible news she had promised them.

Please let me look excited and thrilled, Ruth prayed, as she sat down at the table and looked at her parents across the weathered tabletop. They could barely contain themselves, but they had insisted that she eat first before she told them what she had to say.

With all her possessions in tow, Ruth knew that they expected to hear something about work—probably that she had landed some wonderful job close to home and would be moving back. They had helped her every step of the way in her decision to go to London, but they would be overjoyed were she to tell them that she was returning home.

'I'm not sure where to begin,' Ruth said, when she could no longer postpone the dreaded moment.

She looked at her parents, as wildly dissimilar as two people could be. Her mother was slender and fine-boned, with short fair hair that lent her the same gamine appearance as her daughter. Her father was plump, bordering, as he often said, on beach-ball-shaped. His dark hair was receding faster than he cared to believe and his dark brown eyes were gentle and ironic.

'So I'll just say it in one rush and please don't interrupt till I'm finished.' She drew in a deep breath. 'I met someone a few weeks ago.' She didn't dare look at her parents as she spoke. 'And I fell in love. Problem is, he has a nomadic kind of job. Well, actually, he's a reporter, and he goes away for long periods of time at a stretch.' Uri Geller couldn't bend his spoons more convincingly than she had just bent the truth. 'We hadn't planned on rushing into anything, but...' Here was where the waters got a little choppy. 'But I'm afraid...I was a little bit careless...'

'Darling, you're not...!'

'Which is why we...well, jumped the gun a bit...and got married!' Her voice was thick with a certain unnatural gaiety which fortunately her parents appeared not to notice.

'You're married!' The exclamation, uttered in identical tones of shock, was shrieked in unison, and Ruth raised miserable grey eyes to them.

'I know it's an awful shock...' she said, wringing her hands. 'I wanted to say something...but...'

'But, darling, where *is* he?' Her mother had reached out her hand to Ruth's and was now patting it comfortingly across the remainder of their lunch.

'That's the thing...' Ruth took a deep breath and pleaded with God that she really was doing all this to spare her parents, whom she loved more than anything. So could He please not strike her down just yet with a bolt of lightning? 'He was called away on an urgent matter and he could be gone for weeks… months, even…that's why we rushed into things…'

'Oh, darling, *where*?'

'Where what?' Ruth looked blankly at her parents.

'*Where* has he gone to do his reporting? Is it one of those war-torn countries?'

Ruth, not wanting to get too technical over the details, sought refuge in a forlorn expression and expressed a heartfelt desire not to talk about it.

It was to become her refrain as the days lengthened into one week, then two. Twice she called the office, and the second time she called after hours, leaving a brief message that they should perhaps start thinking about her replacement. Her conscience was unquiet as it was, and lying into an answer-machine somehow seemed less unforgivable than lying to her boss.

Her parents, having ridden the shock of their daughter's pregnancy, had taken to proudly announcing it to all and sundry in the parish, wistfully explaining that the father of the baby was out of the country, risking life and limb for the freedom of others.

Wherever she went she could not escape the well wishes of one and all and constant questions as to her husband's whereabouts.

After a week and a half Ruth had resorted to briefly explaining that her beloved husband was out of telephone contact due to the precariousness of his situation. In time, she knew, the fracas would fade, and she personally couldn't wait. Telling the lie had been monumental enough. Maintaining it threatened to drive her to an early grave.

She was quietly skulking at home, putting the finishing touches to the roast leg of lamb she had prepared for their supper, when she glanced through the kitchen window at the sound of a car crunching up the gravel drive to the house.

A childhood spent in various vicarages had inured her to this—unexpected visits from parishioners at the least appropriate times. Many was the time when grace would have been said and knives and forks raised, and the doorbell would ring.

Her brain half registered the fact that she would now have to stop her preparations and make social small talk for half an hour or so until her parents returned from doing their rounds. She had a fleeting impression of a big car in a dark colour, then the doorbell went. Several short, sharp rings that had her clicking her tongue in annoyance and hurriedly drying her hands so that she could rush to get the door.

She pulled it open, wondering which of her father's elderly fan club members had become so demanding, and the welcoming smile on her face froze.

Her facial muscles, now in a state of paralysis, were quickly joined by the remainder of her body.

'Surprised?' The smoky, sexy voice that had not too long ago been capable of turning her legs to jelly, was cold with contempt. 'Did you think that I wouldn't come looking for you? Did you think that you could run away without explanation and I'd just accept it?'

Ruth gave an involuntary squeak of horror. What was he *doing here*?

He should be…he should be…*he should be in some war-torn country, incommunicado, possibly for ever.*

The possible ramifications of her elaborate lies came

home to roost with terrifying force and she held onto the doorframe to stop herself from collapsing.

She had to get rid of him before her parents returned.

'Inside!' she hissed, pulling him in and then peering outside to see whether there was anyone about. The vicarage, thankfully, was well out of range of passersby, by virtue of its location, set in three acres of sprawling gardens, but there still always seemed to be someone, somewhere, hovering.

'*What* are you doing here?' she demanded, shutting the door and hitting him with the full force of her desperation. She placed her hands squarely on her hips and did her best not to be destabilised by the cold blue eyes looking at her with avenging rage.

Having spent the past three hours in a car, battling with traffic and an eminently unhelpful map, Franco was in no mood for reasonable discussion, even though reasonable discussion was precisely what he had told himself he wanted when he had set out earlier that afternoon.

Naturally, as soon as she opened the door and he saw the face that had driven him crazy for the past few weeks, any possibility of reason had flown through the window. He had been engulfed in a black, smouldering anger that he could feel physically wafting from his body in waves.

It was infuriating enough that he had found himself here, running behind some damned chit of a girl, when every bone in his body had told him that he should just leave the wretch to get on with her life, wherever she chose to live it and with whom. He had never had to wage war with his better judgement and it still galled him to admit that he had lost. He had just not been able to let the things go.

Even more infuriating was the fact that a less remorseful visage he had yet to encounter. If she had been wrapped up in self-pity and regret, ruing the day she walked out on him, ready to plead for entry back into his life, then leniency might have crept in somewhere, but she looked every bit as angry as he felt. And allied to that anger was something else, something he couldn't put his finger on but which could only mean one thing: another man. It was a possibility he didn't dare even contemplate.

'What do you want?' she repeated, casting anxious glances behind him to the closed door.

'Expecting someone, Ruth? My replacement, perhaps?' He gave her a twisted smile.

It occurred to Ruth that arguing was not going to win the war, nor was it going to get rid of him, and get rid of him she must, so she smiled sweetly and forced her posture to relax into something a bit less uptight.

'Look, this isn't a good time. Perhaps if we arranged to meet up later. Maybe tomorrow.'

'I'm not going anywhere until you answer one or two questions.' He pushed himself away from the door and strolled into the hall, looking around him with frank curiosity. 'So this is where you live.'

'How did you find me?' Ruth glanced at her watch and followed a few paces behind him.

'You must have forgotten. You mentioned where you lived the very first time we met. It didn't take long to trace your full address.' He turned around and looked at her. 'Why did you up sticks and leave? I won't begin to tell you how disappointed everyone at the office is with your behaviour. They became worried about you, you know, when they kept telephoning your London number and got nowhere. They had no idea where you lived, because, happily for you, your parents' address had never been recorded on your application form. They all assumed the worst about your mother.'

Ruth blanched. 'I'm sorry...I didn't mean to...'

'To what, Ruth?' His voice was like a whiplash. 'Lie? Deceive people who trusted you? Run away because you couldn't handle what was happening between us? Because that's why you ran away, isn't it?' His blue eyes bored into her until she felt giddy. So far she had experienced no morning sickness during the pregnancy, but right now she felt very nauseous indeed.

'No. You don't understand.' She was almost weeping now. 'You *must* go. Please!'

'Or else what?'

Ruth looked at him helplessly.

'And don't give me that innocent stare!' he exploded. 'Why didn't you wait for me and tell me to my face that you wanted out? Why run away?' He bore down on her and she flinched, faltering back against the wall, pressing herself against it, thankful for the scant support it provided.

'Because I'm a coward!' Ruth babbled. 'I was scared so I did the first craven, cowardly thing I could think of. I ran home to my mum and dad!' Whose absence she fervently hoped would continue just long enough for her to get rid of him.

'You're well rid of me! I'm too gauche for you, too

inexperienced. Do you think that any woman with her wits about her would *run back to her parents the minute she got cold feet*?' She gave a laugh that sounded like a deranged shriek. 'I know this means that you now have no respect for me, but I deserve it! I've behaved abominably. Okay? Is that good enough?' She chewed her bottom lip and frantically willed him to disappear.

This was not what Franco wanted to hear. It reeked of insincerity, although when he thought about it he wasn't too sure *what* he wanted to hear. Something less self-abnegating. But the bottom line was that she was telling him to get lost. She wasn't back in her home town dealing with a broken heart. She had wanted him out of her life and so she had used the quickest method and walked out. Without a backward glance.

He had opened his mouth to give her a piece of his mind, which she richly deserved as far as he was concerned, when there was the sound of fumbling at the front door and two things happened at once.

Ruth gave a groan and sank elegantly to the ground, and a middle-aged couple walked through the door, their chatter drying up on their lips as they absorbed the scene that confronted them.

CHAPTER SEVEN

RUTH opened her eyes to the sight of her mother's worried face inches away from her own, and within seconds the nightmarish memory of *why* she was lying on the ground came flooding back. She gave a short cry of shock and tried to angle her head upwards to see whether Franco really *was* there, or whether it had all been some dreadful figment of her imagination. Some obscure pregnancy symptom, perhaps.

'Darling, now don't try and stand up. Not in your condition...'

'Shh!' Ruth hissed dramatically. She didn't have to look up after all to know that Franco had not been a convenient mirage brought on by a sudden attack of morning sickness. Just behind her mother, two pairs of shoes indicated four feet. Her father's and Franco's. She would have recognised those classy handmade Italian brogues anywhere.

She groaned softly and felt like finding temporary refuge in another attack of the vapours.

'Whatever happened, darling?' Her father's rotund face, now wreathed in lines of concern, joined her mother's, and Ruth smiled weakly at them both.

'I'm afraid that I'm to blame, sir.'

In the fuss after she had passed out, she realised, introductions had not been made. Knowing her parents, they would barely have afforded the stranger a second look after they had seen their daughter swoon-

ing on the floor like a Victorian maiden in a melo-
drama. Now, they both looked up, and there were a
few seconds of silence while they digested the man
who had managed to shift into her line of vision and
was looking down at her with what she loosely inter-
preted as a nasty smile.

She struggled up onto her elbows, frantically trying
to work out what damage limitation exercise she could
adopt, and his hands swiftly pulled her to her feet,
fingers gripping hers hard enough for her to massage
her hand as soon as he had released her.

'Mrs Jacobs, I do apologise for barging into your
house like this.' Franco, all dark, persuasive charm,
extended his hand to the fair-haired woman staring at
him with a perplexed frown. 'How are you feeling?'

'I beg your pardon?'

'Fine!' Ruth inserted, blushing wildly and clasping
her hands behind her back. 'Mum's fine!'

'Ruthie, what *are* you talking about?' her mother
asked, turning to her. 'Have I missed something here?
And shouldn't you be sitting down? We can't have
you falling all over the place, can we?'

'No!' Ruth responded in a high voice. 'Mum, this
is Franco! Now, why don't I take him into the sitting
room and you and Dad can...' her eyes flitted desperately from face to expectant face and settled on her
father's '...can...check the progress of supper! The
lamb's probably burnt to a crisp...!'

Her mother's expression was beginning to look de-
pressingly alert, Ruth noticed, and she slid her arm
around her parents in an attempt to cajole them into
the right direction.

'Ruth...' her mother began to whisper, catching her

eye and smiling delightedly. 'Oh, darling, I'm *so* pleased for you...'

'I'll be back in a moment!' Ruth trilled, pushing her parents towards the kitchen and looking over her shoulder to Franco. 'Just wait in the sitting room, why don't you? It's just through there on the right.'

'Is he who I *think* he is, darling?'

'Who's that? Who's that?' Having safely arrived at the kitchen with both parents in tow, Ruth leaned against the kitchen door and breathed deeply. Surely this had to be a nightmare? In a minute she would open her eyes, discover that it was eight in the morning and everything was as it should be. Real life, after all, didn't have this surreal quality of farce about it.

She sighed and looked at her parents.

'Yes,' she admitted, 'but he won't be staying. He...he...he's in the middle of doing something *terribly* dangerous, very espionage, and he *literally had to sneak out under cover of darkness* to get here. In fact, he was just on his way out when you came home!' The palms of her hands were sweating so profusely that she had to surreptitiously wipe them on her jeans.

'Oh, no!' her mother said with dismay, edging towards the kitchen door—which Ruth resolutely barred.

'Darling, your mother and I really would like to meet your husband, and I'm sure he partly came here to meet us. He seems a fair enough kind of chap...'

'I absolutely refuse to let the man leave until we've at least had a word with him. And why are you behaving so *oddly*? You're as red as a beetroot, Ruthie!'

'I...it's a bit *hot* in the house, Mum,' she stammered, pressing herself against the door.

'Away! Away, away, away!' Her father shooed her, giving her gentle little pushes to dislodge her and then stepping aside so that both females could walk past him.

For the first time ever Ruth speculated on the virtues of running away from home. Twenty-two might seem a bit old to be doing that kind of thing, but then, she thought giddily, how many twenty-two-year-olds had to deal with the horrendous situation staring her in the face?

She would be exposed as a liar in front of her parents and their hearts would be doubly broken. She would never be able to explain why she had lied in the first place and her deepest desire to keep her pregnancy under wraps would be smashed to smithereens. Her only slim hope was to somehow get rid of Franco before either of her parents could blurt out her condition. Perhaps they might imagine that he wasn't aware of it, in which case they would leave it to her to break the news in private.

Franco was lounging in the sitting room by the bay window, staring moodily outside at the impeccably maintained gardens, now shrouded in darkness. He turned around when they entered, his eyes seeking and finding Ruth's with the accuracy of laser-guided missiles.

'Well, old chap,' her father said, beaming. 'Thought we'd never get to meet you!' He strode across and shook Franco's hand vigorously, then he stood back, rocking on his heels, and inspected Franco with paternal thoroughness. 'I gather it's been quite an exercise getting here in the first place!' He patted his shoulder heartily.

''Course, as the father of the most beautiful daughter on the face of the earth, I can happily appreciate why you did your utmost! Now, we *know* you can't stay for long, but surely you can stay long enough to have a quick glass with us…? Some wine, perhaps, or sherry? Might even have a couple of cans of lager—have we got a couple of cans of lager anywhere, darling? So what's it to be…?'

'He'll have the one glass of wine!' Ruth interceded, fairly running across the sitting room and positioning herself next to Franco, with one hand resting warningly on his arm. 'But then he *really must be on his way*. Mustn't you, darling?' She smiled up at him and he shot her a ferociously questioning look.

'Wine would be terrific.'

'Oh, we haven't even introduced ourselves!' Ruth's mother came forward, looking lovingly at her daughter and then transferring her affectionate gaze to Franco. She had a naturally expressive face, quick to smile, and her readiness to see the best in everyone lent her a quality of endearing appeal that few could resist.

'I'm Claire, and that portly chap over there, who absolutely *refuses* to go on a diet, is my husband Michael.'

'I would happily go on a diet, my dear, but I know you would be offended.' He winked at Franco. 'Loves to cook—couldn't bear it if she had no one to experiment on.'

'And Ruth has taken after her in the culinary aspect,' Franco said smoothly, patting the hand that was still resting on his arm and then giving it a squeeze that was unnecessarily firm. 'Hasn't she?'

'The way to a man's heart!' Claire said, laughing. 'Now, cheers to the both of you!'

Ruth, on orange juice only, knocked back her glass with determined speed and then offered a bright smile to no one in particular.

'Now, darlings, I expect you want to spend the last few minutes together, so Dad and I will leave. I *know* we've only exchanged pleasantries,' Claire said seriously, proffering her cheek to be kissed by Franco, 'but I just have a gut feeling that you're going to make an absolutely wonderful son-in-law. Isn't he, Michael?'

'He'd better! Or he'll have me to answer to!'

If Franco was flabbergasted by the revelation of his status, Ruth thought with reluctant admiration, he hid it well. He smiled, murmured one or two polite things, shook hands and then, as soon as her parents were out of the room, turned on Ruth, dropping all semblance of civility.

'Like to tell me what the hell is going on? I feel as though I've walked into a madhouse.'

Her hand dropped from his arm and she nervously took a few steps backwards.

On the plus side, her parents had not breathed a word about her pregnancy. Uncertain as to whether the expectant father knew or not, they had, luckily for Ruth, opted for discretion and silence.

On the minus side, she now faced the uphill task of explaining the inexplicable and, on top of that, persuading Franco to leave with only a fuzzy explanation as to why her parents thought that he was their son-in-law.

'Well?' he growled in a menacing voice, taking

three steps forward to match her two. Ruth backed into the sofa and half fell into a sitting position, watching warily as Franco took up position next to her, uncomfortably close.

It seemed like only yesterday that they had not been able to keep away from each other, touching, feeling, exploring. In another sense all that seemed like an eternity away, part of some youthful game which she had now abandoned for good.

It hurt just to look at him, to breathe him in, to remember.

'Don't even *think* of fainting on me,' he warned silkily, 'or I'll have your parents running in here, and by God I'll drag an explanation out of them as to what the heck's going on around here. So, if you've got any sense at all, you'll keep your wits about you. Got it?'

He stretched his arm out along the back of the sofa and edged threateningly close to her.

'Must you?' she breathed unsteadily.

'Must I *what*?'

'Come so *close*.'

'Why, is this the same Ruth talking? The Ruth who couldn't get close enough to me? The Ruth who once begged to be touched when we were in a restaurant so that we ended up having to leave before the meal was finished?'

'P-Please,' Ruth stammered.

'Please what?' He looked at her grimly, loathing himself for the way those limpid grey eyes could make his stomach clench into knots, even though he knew that he had been taken for a ride.

'Explanation time, darling,' he said softly, shifting into the sofa and flashing her a humourless smile.

'And, contrary to what your parents seem to think, I have all the time in the world to listen to what you have to say.' He crossed his legs and folded his arms behind his head. 'So many questions,' he murmured, 'I hardly know where to begin. Care to help me out there?'

Ruth, frozen into petrified silence, did not respond.

'As I guessed. Well, having come here on a quest to find out why the hell you ran out on me for no apparent reason, I now find that a veritable *nest* of more interesting questions have sprung to life. For instance, *why do your parents think that I'm their son-in-law*?'

'Because...because...' Ruth stared down at her entwined fingers. She could hear her heart thudding madly in her chest, the desperate boom, boom, boom of someone whose options were fast running out.

It was worse than rotten luck that Franco had remembered the one time she had uttered, foolishly, the town where her parents lived. And that he had travelled all the way from London on an explanation-seeking mission to soothe his ego. If he had telephoned she knew that she would have fobbed him off, or at least arranged to meet him somewhere very neutral, where there was no chance of her sweet and blissfully ignorant parents putting in an appearance.

'Because...?' Franco prompted silkily. 'I'm all ears.' There was a thread of sheer menace in his voice that sent a shiver down her spine.

'Because they...it's all a mix-up,' she finally said, clutching at the faint hope that he might believe her. She looked at him evenly and he sighed and shook his head.

'It's no good, you know.'

'What's no good?'

'You trying to lie to me. You just can't do it. Your face gives you away. So why don't you just stop beating about the bush and tell me the truth? Or else your parents are going to find it very perplexing indeed that their daughter has led them to believe that I'm in some frantic rush when in fact I'm still sitting right here when supper's served.'

He rubbed his chin thoughtfully and Ruth realised that he was enjoying all this, enjoying having her at his mercy. She supposed she had done the unforgivable—walked away from a man who had probably never suffered the indignity of being dumped in his life before.

'I suppose...' he drawled with shark-like relish, 'that I could always *ask* your good parents to tell me what this is all about...'

'No! Okay, I'll tell you.' She took a deep breath and then said in a rush, 'They think you're their son-in-law because I told them that we were married.'

'Well, *obviously* that's why they think I'm their son-in-law. The question is *why have you lied to them*?'

He looked at her narrowly, at the slender hands twining miserably on her lap, at the impossibly fair hair framing her delicate face, at the varying shades of colour tingeing her cheeks, giving away her discomfort.

Well, quite frankly, she couldn't be too uncomfortable for his liking. Something was afoot. All would be revealed in due course, but, for the while, he was remarkably content to watch her squirm under his questions and beady-eyed gimlet stare.

It was all the more satisfying since—against all reason, considering the way she had walked out on him without a backward glance—he still had a compelling desire to touch her, to stroke her, to make love to her.

Thank God her parents were in the house. He had a sickening suspicion that if they hadn't been he would have been sorely tempted to let his hands and mouth do some of the arguing on his behalf. Which would have inevitably met with rejection. It was a thought he found impossible to contemplate.

'Please go,' Ruth whispered, without bothering to try and think of a reasonable explanation. There *was* no reasonable explanation. All she could do now was to appeal to his better nature, and she knew that he *had* a better nature. Despite his air of formidable self-confidence, and despite the fact that he had an uncanny talent for appearing utterly and calmly in control of every possible situation, she knew that he was kind and humorous and thoughtful in ways that could be incredibly unexpected.

And really, for the sake of the good times they had shared, surely he would leave her alone if she asked, if he could see how much it meant to her?

It wasn't as though she was the beginning, the middle and the end of his universe. However intense their relationship had been, it had been brief, and if *she* had emerged scarred from the experience, then he was intact.

If she could somehow persuade him not to let his curiosity get the better of him, then perhaps he would go away quietly and she could keep her secret safely hidden.

'Now, why would I do that?' he asked, pouring

himself the remainder of the wine from the wine bottle which her father had left on the coffee table in front of the sofa, 'when things here are so riveting?'

'Because,' Ruth said, meeting his relentless blue eyes without flinching, 'it would please me. I'm sorry I lied to them, it was a mistake, but if you would just leave and not look back, then it's a mistake that can be remedied.'

A dark flush spread through his face and he swallowed the contents of his glass savagely, then banged the glass on the table and looked at her.

'No,' he returned coldly. 'My name's been played with and I am owed an explanation. And if *you* won't provide it, then I'm sure your parents would be more than happy to oblige.' He began standing up and Ruth feverishly pulled him back down.

'Okay. I'll tell you.' She looked at him tremulously. 'I'm pregnant.'

The word dropped between them like a hand grenade. Ruth, eyes squeezed tightly shut, waited for the fall-out.

When there was no loud explosion of rage, she tentatively opened her eyes and immediately realised that an explosion would have been preferable to the shocked stillness of the man sitting next to her. Her revelation had rendered him speechless in the worst possible way.

A tear drizzled to the corner of her eye and she wiped it with the back of her hand. There was to be none of that. It mattered not that any number of horrendous complications could ensue from his awareness of the situation—the first involving her parents, who were currently innocently chatting in the kitchen, unaware of what was to come.

'You're pregnant,' he said flatly, standing up and walking across to the bay window. Putting, she thought bleakly, as much distance now between them.

'I wasn't going to tell you...' Ruth began in a shaky voice. 'It was a mistake...'

'But we were using contraception,' he said harshly.

'But not the first time.' She got up and quietly shut the door to the sitting room. The last thing she needed was for her parents to witness unnecessarily a slanging match between their daughter and so-called son-in-law.

'I know that maybe I should have told you...'

'No.' His voice dripped with glacial sarcasm. 'Why should you? The fact that you're carrying *my* baby is only a minor detail that really hasn't got much to do with me at all, isn't it.'

'Can you blame me?' Ruth's eyes flashed with sudden anger.

'Yes, I damn well can, as a matter of fact!' His eyes smouldered with rage. She could feel it emanating from him across the length of the room, suffocating her.

'Why? Why?' she cried, leaning forward. 'What's so difficult for you to understand?'

'Are you a *fool*?'

'No, I'm not!' She could barely speak because her voice was so unsteady. 'As far as I was concerned, I was doing you a favour!' She glared at him, and all of a sudden the strange calm that had carried her along for the past few weeks shattered into oblivion. The starkly grim reality of what was happening to her was like a blow to the stomach.

This was no ordinary situation. With the best possible intentions in the world, she had lied to her parents and had stupidly involved Franco in the lie. Now he could blow the whole thing apart. They lived in a small village where the parishioners would not be backward in passing judgement on the vicar and his unwed, pregnant daughter. Not only would *she* suffer, but so might her parents, two people who had done nothing but believe the story their daughter had fabricated.

'*When first we practise to deceive…*' Why, oh, why hadn't she remembered that at the time? She should have told him everything. Now, in trying to conceal it all, she risked the worst possible outcome.

'You and I…we had a fling. A baby was not part of the agenda, and when I found out that I was pregnant, I suppose I just…panicked. I couldn't imagine that you would want a baby in your life and I had no intention of…getting rid of it. I just thought that the easiest thing to do would be to leave, let you get on with your life.

'I lied to my parents because I was a coward. I *am* a coward. It would have broken their hearts if they had known…the truth, that I was pregnant and unmarried. I know it happens all the time, and they wouldn't have flung me out the house and told me never to darken their door again, but they're old-fashioned, and it would have been tough on them what with Dad being the vicar.'

'And what did you intend to tell your parents when your husband failed to make an appearance? Misplaced your address, perhaps! Had second thoughts about the whole thing? Or maybe you painted him as some kind of inveterate bum whom you'd idiotically married on a whim?'

'I hadn't thought that far ahead,' Ruth whispered. 'I suppose I might have killed you off.'

'Killed me off?'

'Well, you *were* involved in a dangerous line of business.'

'What? What line of business?' He came back to the sofa and sat down heavily.

'Reporting from war zones.'

'What?' He resisted the urge to burst out laughing. There was nothing funny about the situation, but her ingenuity amused him. 'Any in particular?' he asked pleasantly. 'Or just the most life-threatening?'

'I hadn't specified. What are you going to do?' She raised her eyes to his and looked at him steadily.

'Well, here's what I'm *not* going to do,' he informed her bluntly. 'I won't be walking away from my responsibilities; that's the first thing. So, whether you like it or not, you'll be seeing me on a regular basis from now on. You lied to your parents about my fictional hair-raising occupation so you can un-lie your way out of that one. As for our status as husband and wife—well, I'll have to think about how I decide to deal with that...'

'But...' She frowned as the innumerable complicated permutations of that particular lie sprang to mind. 'You can't hang around...people will wonder why we don't live under the same roof if we're married.'

He shrugged. 'Well, you can work on that, can't

you? You're so gifted in the art of fabrication, you should be able to come up with something...' He stood up and flexed his muscles, rubbing the back of his neck. 'So why don't we go and see your parents? They'll be thrilled when they realise that I won't have to go rushing off after all, won't they?'

He politely allowed her to lead the way, maintaining a telling silence, while his brain whirred with the connotations of what she had just told him.

He was going to be a father. *He was going to be a father!* He didn't know whether he felt deliriously happy or abjectly terrified, or whether he just felt bloody confused, but the one thing he *did* know was that the ground had very neatly been pulled out from under his feet.

When he thought of the fact that none of this would have been revealed had he not made the journey to find her, he felt the blood rush to his head. He was consumed by a rage that was so pure and undistilled that it seemed to have enough force to blow him off his feet.

His baby! So what if he had never indicated an interest in fatherhood? So what if he had always implied that his life was just too full for the responsibilities that came with a family? Was that any reason for her to keep the fact of her pregnancy hidden?

She turned to give him a brief, hesitant look as the sound of her parents' voices reached their ears, and he frowned coolly at her.

They would have beautiful children.

A beautiful child. He instantly corrected the errant thought.

'Franco. Have you come to say goodbye? Such a

shame that you have to disappear just when we were getting to know one another.' Claire walked over to where he was standing by the doorway and reached out her hands to him in a gesture of warmth and acceptance.

At that, he gave Ruth, who was busy contemplating this scene, a meaningful look, and she cleared her throat and said, in a high-pitched voice, 'Actually, Mum, Franco might be able to stay for supper with us.'

As expected, her mother's face broke into a radiantly pleased smile, and, without ado, she drew him into the kitchen and sat him at the table. From behind him she made lots of mouthing motions to Ruth which were clearly visible as *Have you told him about the baby?* and Ruth, unsure where things were going now, wore the baffled expression of someone conversing with a mad person and pretended to misunderstand.

What if he revealed everything? The marriage that never was, the love that didn't exist, the fling that had more to do with sex than anything else? Would her mother believe *her* if she then proceeded to talk about love and how meaningful it had been for *her*? Or would she emerge as a cheap tart who had fallen prey to stupidity?

For the millionth time her mind drifted away as she contemplated a future of parental disappointment and social ostracism.

She snapped back to the present to hear Franco charmingly informing her parents that he would be staying for longer than merely supper, and she shut her half-opened mouth with a snap.

'W-what did you say?' she stammered, looking at

him and trying to work out what that self-satisfied expression on his face was all about.

'I *said*—' he smiled, catching her eye and beckoning her over with his finger '—that my brief visit might well extend to something a bit...more substantial.' He patted his lap and Ruth blushed furiously, confused as to what that gesture was supposed to mean.

Out of the corner of her eye she saw her parents exchange knowing winks and was further mortified.

'More substantial?'

The patting of the lap now bordered on a silent command, and Ruth reluctantly went across to where he was sitting and primly perched on his lap.

'Isn't it wonderful? Darling?' His lips nuzzled the nape of her neck and she brushed the tingling sensation away with one hand.

'Wonderful. Hang on, Mum, let me give you a hand with those things.' Her heart was slamming against her ribcage. She couldn't figure out what he was playing at and her uncertainty was nerve-racking.

'So, how did you manage to wangle that?' her father asked, beaming. Both her parents were beaming. It was enough to make you sick.

'One or two phone calls,' Franco said mysteriously. 'After all, now that *fatherhood* is on the way, I can hardly leave my blushing bride to cope on her own, can I?'

'I wouldn't want you to abandon your duties,' Ruth returned quickly, slamming the dishes on the table until she caught her father's eye and adopted a less aggressive approach to the table-setting. 'After all, you know how *stimulating* you find what you do.'

'Well, yes. Working as a top reporter in some of the most dangerous hotspots in the world *is* stimulating, but...' He reached out and stilled her frantic hand, stroking it and then giving it a gentle squeeze. 'What could be more stimulating than being by your wife's side so that you can witness the creation of new life?'

'How long are you planning on staying?' Ruth asked, appalled by the way events appeared to be unfolding. She took the platter of lamb from her mother and deposited it on the table.

'Oh, I think I can stay for at least a few weeks...'

'*A few weeks?*'

'That's wonderful!' Claire said brightly, giving her daughter a brief hug in passing. 'Isn't that tremendous news, Ruthie?'

'But what about your...*job*?' She turned to her parents and said, a little wildly, 'Franco just does the odd bit of troubleshooting. In fact, he also works in an off...sorry, has a company.'

'What company would that be?' her father asked, and Franco gave a self-deprecating shrug of his broad shoulders.

'Just a few small concerns...one of them is practically a hobby, isn't it, my darling?'

'Won't those *small concerns* miss you if you stagnate here in the middle of nowhere for weeks on end?' Ruth hissed, infuriated by the smile tugging the corners of his mouth.

'Oh, I can pop up now and again to check on things! And I can bring my laptop here.' He turned to her father. 'Computers have shrunk the world, wouldn't you say? If I wanted to, I could probably do most of my business from one room in a house, provided I had the right equipment around me! Have computers reached religion as yet?' He settled comfortably in the chair with every appearance of someone getting used to surroundings they had no plans on leaving in a hurry.

'Dear boy—' her father leant forward, warming to his pet subject '—you'd be surprised. Bit of a computer boffin myself, actually.' He winked at his daughter. 'Good to have a man around to discuss it with…'

CHAPTER EIGHT

IT HAD been the longest dinner Ruth had ever endured. The lavish meal of roast lamb with all the trimmings appeared to be incidental to the main business of Franco winning her parents over.

Every mouthful of food had been punctuated with some fascinating evidence of wit and charm, and by the time she and her mother had begun clearing the table her parents had been hooked and reeled in like two helpless flounders.

She had tried her utmost not to catch his eye, but whenever she had she'd been rewarded with a look that promised a *very long chat* on the subject of her pregnancy.

At least, though, her parents, misinformed as they were, had not seen their illusions shattered, and for that she owed him a debt of gratitude. The question still remained: *what happens next?*—she had no doubt that he would fill her in on that without sparing her feelings. Making life easy for her was not, she suspected, at the top of his list of *must dos*.

And really, in a way, it was almost a relief to have everything in the open with him. Her decision to run away, necessary though it had seemed at the time, had encrusted her soul with a layer of ice and turned her into someone she didn't much like. Deception had never been a trait she admired, and to have succumbed so completely to it herself, whatever the circumstances, had made her feel sick inside herself.

She sighed and thought that the only passably good thing to have emerged from the evening was the fact that Franco would not be sharing her room with her. It had given her a surge of pleasure to say, with regret in her voice, that her bed, like the bed in the two free bedrooms, was of a single size. She didn't know if she had the strength to lie next to Franco's blatantly masculine body without reaching out to touch him, and that would be a disaster. She had forfeited any passing claim she had ever made on his affections.

Right now he should be safely ensconced in the small bedroom down the corridor from her, with the sloping roof and the patchwork quilt. He was so tall that his feet would stick out at the bottom of the bed and he would probably spend the night tossing and turning and trying to get into a comfortable position. He was not accustomed to small dimensions. His bed in his apartment in London was of the king sized variety. Enough room to hold a party.

Unfortunately, or fortunately, in this instance, the myriad rooms in the vicarage had mostly been turned into other things. One of the unused bedrooms had been turned into her father's office, one had been converted into a sewing room for her mother, and another two housed various *projects* which the parishioners seemed to have on the go on a fairly regular basis.

It wasn't unusual for Ruth to stroll into one of these rooms and be confronted by a barrage of hand-knitted stuffed dolls, waiting patiently for some charity fair or other and staring at the door with blank, woolly eyes, or else a vast assortment of brightly coloured cushions which seemed to be crying out for the addition of nubile girls in harem outfits.

The sheer eccentric chaos would get to him after a while. After, she suspected, a very short while. That, and the boredom of small village life, where eating out at a decent restaurant involved a forty-five minute trek into the nearest large town and the main topics of conversation were not stocks and shares but roses, manure and the weather.

In the darkness of her bedroom, she smirked to herself.

She was revolving in her head what other aspects of village life would get up his nose when there was a brief knock on the door, then it was pushed open, and, outlined against the light from the corridor, was Franco. A dark, well-built silhouette wearing a pair of boxer shorts and a tee shirt which he had borrowed from her father.

She realised that she wasn't surprised to see him. She had more than half expected it. Was that why she had abandoned her favoured night gear of skimpy vest and little shorts and opted for the one flannelette nightie she possessed?

He had retreated to his bedroom at a little after ten-thirty with the docility of a lamb, having trapped her into walking up the stairs with him but unable to prevent her from scampering back downstairs before they could make it to the isolated confines of his bedroom. His last words had been *Later, my darling*, which had barely made her steps falter.

The threatening little syllables had obviously been lodged somewhere in the forefront of her brain, though, because her eyes barely flickered now when she saw him.

Without saying a word, she switched on her bedside lamp and watched in silence as he pushed himself away from the doorframe and sauntered into the bedroom, carefully closing the door behind him. He had obviously waited until he assumed her parents to be asleep. Their bedroom was well within earshot of raised voices.

A little shiver of awareness slithered through her as he sat on the side of her bed, depressing the mattress with his weight. That, she thought gloomily, was the snake in the grass. It didn't matter how much she reasoned things out on a logical basis, how much she told herself that it would be a huge relief when he abandoned her as an object of revenge for walking out on him and, even worse, walking out on him when she was carrying his baby, she still felt an electric thrill whenever he was around. In fact, the past few weeks seemed to have been lived in cotton wool, and now that he was in the house and threatening to get under her skin she felt truly alive again.

Of course, that didn't mean that she *really wanted him around*, she reasoned to herself, screwing up her life for all the wrong reasons.

'I know you're going to shout at me,' she began defensively, 'and there's no point. It might make you feel better but it won't change anything.' Despite the fact that she had semi-rehearsed these lines, she still failed to sound firm and convincing. In fact, she was only a hair's breadth away from subsiding into a nervous stutter.

'Shout at you? Wake your parents up after they've

been so welcoming and hospitable? Perish the thought.' He smiled at her and she shivered.

'Thank you,' she said, looking away, 'for not...'

'Exposing their shy, unassuming daughter for the inveterate liar that she is?'

'I'm not an inveterate liar,' Ruth said mutinously.

'No? Well, it doesn't matter now. What matters is how we intend to deal with all of this.'

'We could have talked about it in the morning. There was no need for you to come here tonight.' As a form of protest, it sounded pretty unconvincing to her ears, considering he'd now been sitting on her bed for a good ten minutes.

'Oh, but you're my *wife*. I can do whatever I please with you!'

Ruth reddened and drew her knees up to her chest under the quilt, dragging it up, then she hugged her legs and rested her chin on her knees. 'You know that's not true,' she said in a faltering voice.

His eyes caught hers and her pulse began to beat with a quickened, steady pace.

'Well, we'll leave that for the moment, shall we?' Another one of those smiles that made her nervous system go into overdrive. 'Let's talk about the immediate future.'

'You can't possibly stay here for weeks on end,' Ruth said, with a question in her voice.

'Why not?'

'Because you've got things to do in London.'

'Yes, well, as it transpires, I've got things to do here as well.'

Her grey eyes glinted in the mellow light and, involuntarily, his eyes dropped to the slender column of her neck and the slight body bulked out by the quilt. She was wearing a thick nightgown. Nothing like she used to wear in bed with him.

To his lasting amusement, she had always refused to sleep naked, blaming it on her upbringing, but her nightclothes had never been of the granny variety. Baggy boxer shorts and loose white vests that always showed the twin peaks of her breasts, pushing against the cotton like pointed buds, begging to be touched. His eyes shot back to her face and he frowned.

'Would you ever have told me?' he asked quietly. 'Or would you happily have allowed my child to be born into this world without ever knowing the identify of its father?'

Ruth felt her mouth go dry. 'I hadn't really thought about it,' she whispered truthfully.

'You hadn't really thought about *anything*, had you?' He knew that he was beating this to death, but he couldn't help himself. She had been quite happy to go it alone! In fact, he thought darkly, she had probably been enjoying her independence before he showed up on the scene, while *he*, on the other hand, man of the world, eligible bachelor infamous Houdini when it came to the opposite sex, had spent *weeks* torn apart by her absence from his life.

'I thought I was doing the right thing.'

'The *right* thing? Surely, as a vicar's daughter, you *must* know that the last thing you were doing was the *right thing*!' He could feel himself on the verge of exploding and was obliged to surreptitiously take a few deep breaths to regain some self-control.

Think of the nightgown, he told himself with grim satisfaction. She was wearing what could only be called the ultimate man deterrent. Because, he decided, *because* just in case he showed up, which she had half expected him to, judging from her lack of outrage, she didn't want to be clad in anything remotely sexy. Because the thought of sex and him still did something for her. Still, he decided, *turned her on.*

'All right, then, the *best* thing.'

'For whom? The best thing *for whom*?' He watched as her fingers plucked nervously at the quilt cover and she licked her lips. Then she straightened her legs, revealing the true depth of her sexless nightwear in all its splendid *spinster aunt* glory.

It had all the hallmarks of sexlessness. A ruffled neckline, a few little pearl buttons down the front, long sleeves. Probably reached to her ankles as well, he thought, staring at her face yet, mysteriously, still managing to see the swell of her breasts under the unrevealing cloth. He felt himself harden and adjusted his sitting position accordingly.

'For…everyone…'

'Tomorrow…' he said, getting up and strolling across to the window, out of which he proceeded to stare before turning to face her tense figure on the bed. Her hands, demurely linked on her lap, fidgeted continually. 'Tomorrow I intend to go to London to sort out one or two things. I'll probably be there a couple of days, then I'll be back. With clothes. And while I'm gone you'll have to do a little bit of furniture replacement.' He moved across to the bed, where he proceeded to tower over her prone form, his fingers fractionally tucked into the elasticised waistband of the boxer shorts.

'What do you mean?'

'You know what I mean,' Franco said on a long-suffering sigh. 'This sleeping arrangement isn't going to work. For starters, what are your parents going to think? That your besotted husband, fresh back from those war zones, is content to sleep in a separate room from his coy, young wife?' He looked at her with hooded eyes. 'No.' He shook his head, 'As your husband, I have one or two rights…'

Ruth felt her heart begin to flutter madly. Wasn't this taking the game too far? But how on earth could she complain without giving everything away?

'I can't redecorate my parents' house,' she attempted feebly, and he sprang onto her reply with alacrity.

'In which case we could always move out. Get a cosy little flat somewhere. Or a house. Yet, flats are for the city; houses are much more what we'd want here, in the middle of this beautiful countryside. Something small and ivy-clad, perhaps a thatched roof.'

'You've been looking at too many chocolate box covers,' Ruth declared, with a sniff. 'Houses like that don't exist in this part of the world.' She found herself drifting into a very pleasant world of Franco, the baby and cosy evenings spent in front of a roaring log fire in some wonderful, fictitious thatched cottage, and metaphorically pinched herself back to the present.

'Why are you doing this?' she asked, looking at him. How could a man look so obscenely spectacular in an oversized tee shirt with a cartoon logo on the front? It wasn't fair. Little wonder she had stupidly fallen in love with him. He was the type of man who was positively lethal when it came to virginal country girls with marginal experience of men and a head full of romantic dreams.

'What's the alternative?' he asked smoothly. He had known that she would ask him that question sooner or later, and the truth was that his answer had been a little too long in coming for his liking.

He might well rage and rant and hurl accusations at her, but the facts were straightforward enough. She was pregnant and had involved him in a lie to spare her parents a small part of the truth. Well, even if it hadn't occurred to her, it had certainly occurred to him that everyone could emerge a winner from the situation.

All he had to do was go along with the lie for a while, perhaps disappear on some fictitious mission, reappearing when the baby was born and thereafter vanishing again until it became clear that his presence was not a constant and a divorce was inevitable.

Seeing the child would be no problem because he could simply persuade her to move back to London, perhaps even hand her back her job with a few more perks thrown in so that she had ample money, and visits could happily occur during the week or on weekends. End of complicated story.

However, this version of possible events was not what he discovered he wanted.

He didn't want to be a part-time father and a pretend husband. He wanted more than that, although whenever he got to that point in his head he firmly switched off rather than meander down the twisty road to its shady, unwelcome destination.

He watched her face closely in the semi-darkness

and had to resist the urge to hurry the conversation along until it got to the point he wanted.

'You could always go away,' she suggested timidly. 'I mean, I wouldn't try and stop you from seeing the baby whenever you wanted...'

'No can do. You involved me in this and I don't intend to emerge from it looking like a cad and a bounder.'

'Who would know?' Ruth asked, trying to follow his train of thought.

'Every single friend I possess, for a start. I mean, Ruth, *think about it*. I'm a single man one minute, and the next minute I'm visiting a baby, having abandoned the mother to her own devices. And what about your parents? Eh? *Their* opinion of me is hardly going to be sky-high when I vanish off the face of the earth leaving you to get on with things on your own.' *Why* that mattered, *exactly*, was hard to say, but matter it did.

'You could always pay child maintenance if that makes you feel better.'

'*No!*'

'Shh! You'll wake my parents. They're very light sleepers!'

'No.' He lowered his voice but didn't alter its tone. 'Doesn't it make more sense for me to go along with this and for things to taper off if needs be?'

If needs be? he thought. What does *that* mean? Why did his vocal cords insist on forming ridiculous sentences that had nothing to do with his thought processes?

'If needs be? What does that mean?'

'It means,' he said heavily, 'that I intend to be

around for a while and there's nothing you can do about it.' He stood up and looked down at her, challenging her to question his decision further, ready for any verbal fight she might care to indulge in, but she seemed bemused by the course of events.

'Just make sure,' he said, turning to her, his hand on the doorknob, 'that you get the bed.'

Which was a request that she found nigh on impossible to obey.

Like the devoted husband he wasn't he called her every evening for the five nights he was away, making sure, she suspected, that he called at dinner time, when he knew that her parents would be around. Why, she had no idea. If his sojourn in her life was to be temporary, why go to any lengths to impress her parents, two people he would never see again?

It made no sense, and she quickly decided that she was reading meaning into something basically meaningless. He called at the same time every evening because it was the most convenient time for him *to* call.

Which left quite a bit of free time, she thought. What did he get up to after eight in the evening? Back home to his apartment to sit in front of the telly with a pre-packaged meal for one on his lap? Hardly. But, if not, then where *was* he?

On the night before he was due to return, Ruth finally gave in to impulse and dialled his home number. She was so utterly convinced that he would be out, living down to her worst suspicions, that she was flabbergasted when the telephone was answered and she heard his dark, velvety voice down the end of the line.

'It's me,' she blurted out, and then added hastily, in case he didn't recognise her voice, 'Ruth.'

'I *know* who it is. What's the matter? Is everything all right?' His voice was laced with sudden, urgent anxiety and Ruth allowed herself a moment of sheer pleasure during which she indulged in the brief but sweetly tempting fantasy that Franco actually *cared* about her.

'Yes! Nothing's wrong with the baby. I'm fine.'

There was a small, telling pause.

'Then why are you calling?'

'I'm sorry,' Ruth said stiffly. 'Am I interrupting anything?'

'Depends…'

'Oh, I see.' She saw a tall, leggy glamorous woman sitting at the rough, incredibly expensive hand-made dining table, swirling a glass of champagne in one hand, long raven-black hair falling in a mass of curls over one shoulder, smouldering Latin eyes thickly fringed, promising him who knew what antics in the bedroom later that night.

'I've just this minute got back from work, actually.'

'At this hour?' Ruth heard her voice rise in suspicious disbelief, and she cleared her throat and continued with ghastly formality, 'You must be exhausted. I'm sorry I disturbed you.'

'Forget it.'

In the background she heard the clink of ice being tossed into a glass. He was on the mobile, probably in the exquisitely and rarely used high-tech kitchen. She strained her ears to see whether she could discern another lot of clinking ice which would be a telltale sign that he had company, but there was nothing, and she found herself momentarily breathing a sigh of relief.

'You never said what you wanted.' He spoke into

her ear, and for a wild moment she imagined that she could almost feel his breath against her cheek.

'Nothing!'

The one telling word was out before she could take it back, and she heard a dry chuckle down the end of the line. 'You mean you were just missing me?'

'I was doing no such thing!'

'Then perhaps you wanted to check my where-abouts. Could you have become seized with a sudden attack of jealousy because I wasn't around?'

His wild but accurate stab at the truth made her give a forced cackle of laughter.

'Don't be ridiculous. You have an ego the size of...the size of...'

'C'mon, Ruth, can't you think of anything else I have that's as big as my so-called ego?'

She felt her face begin to burn as her mind swerved off obligingly in the direction he had pointed to, only skidding to an abrupt halt when he said, with amuse-ment, 'You're blushing, aren't you? I can feel it down the line.'

'Oh!' She made a few strangled sounds under her breath. 'I just *called* as a *matter of fact*—' at last, inspiration! '—to tell you that I've wasted hundreds of valuable man hours tramping through the nearest towns in search of a wretched bed that can be deliv-ered by tomorrow and...' She allowed a few seconds to elapse, thoroughly, and childishly enjoying the an-ticipation of satisfaction about to come. 'The earliest any double bed can be delivered is in four weeks' time.'

'No problem. Leave it with me.'

'Leave it with you? And what can *you* do that I

can't?' Her moment of triumph had lasted the length of time it took for her to blink.

'You'd be pleasantly surprised. I'll make sure it's delivered by tomorrow afternoon.' His voice dropped a couple of notches. 'Aren't you excited, darling? We'll be able to sleep together! The way we should...seeing that we're married now...' He gave a throaty chuckle, and she slammed the receiver down.

She'd worked it out. At long last, she'd worked it out, and it amazed her that she hadn't slotted the pieces of the jigsaw together before now.

Yes, he wanted to take responsibility in the matter of the baby, but Franco Leoni was a charming, sexy, self-confident predator when it came to the opposite sex, and he intended to stick around and take full advantage of the situation in which he found himself, to continue sleeping with her. He still wanted her and he intended to have her, until he grew tired and bored with his conquest, at which point, and not a minute before, he would do his convenient vanishing act, only reappearing at intervals to do his fatherly duties.

There was nothing she could do about it. In public, he had licence to do whatever he pleased. He could touch her, stand as close to her as he liked, allow his hands to wander wherever they wanted, within reason, and she had unwittingly handed him this freedom.

And in private...

Ruth shivered and began heading up the stairs to the bedroom and the short-lived comfort of her single bed.

He knew that she was still attracted to him. Her body and face revealed as much even if her mouth insisted on paying lip service to politeness.

What if a bed *did* arrive tomorrow?

She pushed open the door to her bedroom and stared forlornly at her conveniently sized bed for one. She had visions of the two of them, back to sharing a bed, their bodies touching even if she tried to edge to the furthest part of the bed as possible. He knew how to touch her; he could break her in a matter of seconds....

'How wonderful!'

Those were her mother's words as the lorry backed up the drive to deliver the bed.

'I can think of plenty more wonderful things,' Ruth muttered under her breath.

'What's that, dear? How did he *manage* to get this all sorted out in a matter of a few hours?' Her mother had taken charge of the situation and was crisply giving instructions and leading the way up the stairs to the bedroom. 'And such a marvellous bed, as well! I've always longed for a wrought-iron bed.' She sighed dreamily and Ruth was sorely tempted to tell her mother that she could have the thing, no charge. 'There's something terribly *romantic* about a wrought-iron bed, wouldn't you agree, darling?'

'No. I prefer wood myself.'

Her mother peered back over her shoulder to give her a chiding look. 'I hope you won't be indiscreet enough to tell that to your husband!' she scolded. 'He must have spent *hours* choosing this and arranging the whole thing.'

'Mum, he probably spent five minutes on the phone!'

'He must be awfully persuasive in that case.' They watched in silence for a few minutes as the delivery men wrestled with the base of the bed through the door of the bedroom. The single bed had been ignominiously put in one of the outbuildings a couple of hours before by her father and three of the parishioners, who had needed quite some cups of tea to recover from the exertion.

'It's called rich, I think.'

'Now, Ruth, it's not like you to be cynical. Franco is a delightful man and he clearly adores you. Super! Could you just shift it a tiny bit more towards the centre? Yes, just right! Ruth! Come and have a peek!'

'It's very nice,' Ruth admitted grudgingly. She didn't dare step too far into the room. It was bad enough seeing the vast expanse of double bed that seemed to be mocking her crumbling sensibilities from halfway behind her mother's back outside the bedroom.

'Are you excited?' Her mother turned to her and giggled.

'No, I am not!' Ruth said severely. 'I mean...I mean...'

'Yes, I *know* it won't be the first time, but there's something so *precious* about my baby girl, married and sharing a bed with her husband. I can still remember when you hated boys, for goodness' sake!'

Ruth belatedly wished that she had continued to pursue that path.

'Oh, Mum. Please!'

Claire affectionately gave her daughter a hug and they watched the delivery men depart with wildly different thoughts going through their heads.

The so-called divorce, Ruth was fast realising, coming after the so-called marriage, would hit her parents hard. Much harder now that they had met the so-called husband and had had a chance to like him. She sighed with a mixture of frustration and sheer worry.

'I know.' Her mother patted her arm and ushered her back into the house. 'You feel a bit misty-eyed as well, don't you?' They strolled into the kitchen while Claire continued to prattle on with whimsy about childhood and getting older.

'You wait until you have your own,' she said knowingly, as she filled the kettle and spooned coffee into two mugs. 'I only wish, you know, that your dad and I could have had a big wedding for you. Or at least had *something*.

This niggling, guilt-inducing line of conversation had reared its head soon after Ruth had arrived back with her news weeks previously, and she was disconcerted that it was surfacing once again.

'I mean, darling, I *do* understand. Franco had to dash away without any notice at all and you simply had to leap at the chance or risk missing it altogether, but still...'

'I know, Mum. If things could have been a bit different, then, well, you know I would have loved to have had a white wedding. A very *small* white wedding... But, you know, sometimes things just don't work out the way we expect them to...'

She relieved her mother of the mug of coffee and took a couple of sips, then headed for the larder and the biscuit tin. Disappointingly, the chocolate bourbons had all been eaten. She would have to have a word with her dad about that. Hadn't he promised to stay away from the biscuits?

She returned to the kitchen to find her mother waiting for her with an unnerving glint in her eye.

'Darling, I've had a wonderful idea.'

'Yes?' Ruth asked warily, edging back into her chair and making do with the custard creams.

'You know we were talking about how disappointed we both were that there was no white wedding…?'

Ruth hadn't realised that she had ever mentioned any such thing, but she nodded obligingly anyway.

'Well…' The smile on her mother's face made her look like a girl of sixteen. 'What about a *blessing*? Just something right here, in the vicarage. Something terribly informal. We could ask a few of the parishioners. You *know* how fond they all are of you…and now that Franco is going to be around for a little while…well, I'm *sure* he'd be delighted with the idea…!'

'Delighted with what idea?'

Both women swung around at the sound of Franco's voice from the kitchen doorway.

'No idea,' Ruth burst out. 'Mum was just…' She caught her mother's eye and lapsed into sulky silence.

'Come in here, Franco. You look exhausted. I'll make you a cup of coffee and tell you all about *my wonderful idea*!'

CHAPTER NINE

'How could you?' Ruth watched stormily as Franco strolled towards the ridiculously huge double bed and proceeded to test the mattress. He kicked off his shoes, rolled up the sleeves of his shirt and, after bouncing on the bed a few times, lay down with his legs crossed and his arms folded behind his head.

'Incredibly comfortable,' he informed her, ignoring the look of outrage on her face and allowing his eyes to roam lazily over her. 'Not too hard, not too soft. Goldilocks would have a field-day on this one. Even *with* the three bears towering over her, she'd still be inclined to stay put.'

She was, he thought delightedly, positively *vibrating* with dismay at the way he had grabbed her mother's idea and gone along with the concept, lock, stock and barrel. She obviously had not the slightest idea how delicious she looked, standing there in the doorway, hands on hips, body thrust belligerently forward, her blonde hair swinging across her face and her perfect mouth downturned. How could any sane man be expected to hold a normal conversation with a woman who was so immensely provocative without even realising it?

The pair of jeans, which fitted snugly on her frame, were too long, and had been roughly cuffed at the bottom where there was just a sliver of teasing, slender ankle peeping out before a pair of inappropriately fluffy bedroom slippers took over. The checked shirt, which might have looked unappealing on any other women, *radiated* sexuality on this one, and Franco indulged himself by staring at her, taking it all in, enjoying every minute of his inspection.

He could well imagine her breasts underneath, clad in one of those functional stretchy Lycra bras she seemed to prefer wearing, the kind that were designed to do nothing for a man's imagination except perhaps squash it. But gazing at her breasts contoured beneath the sporty elasticised fabric had brought him a thrill that no lacy bra on any woman had ever succeeded in doing in his life before. One very short meander down memory lane and he could conjure up the image without any difficulty at all.

'Are you going to say *anything* or are you just going to *lie there*?' Ruth spluttered, pink-faced.

'I'm just going to lie here,' he replied seriously, watching as her face went a shade brighter.

When he had first arrived at the vicarage, unannounced and seething with what he considered well-justified rage, he had expected no more than a brief but explosive showdown at the end of which he had planned on leaving with his mind well and truly satisfied. He had reluctantly but eventually given in to his insane desire to see her one last time and *find out why she had run out on him*, but he had had every intention of making sure that he left with the last word.

It still mystified him that she had managed to bewitch him right back into feeling those old, inconvenient feelings which he had spent weeks stuffing away in a cupboard labelled *soft*.

He couldn't look at her without feeling desire, and

he couldn't listen to a word she said without being utterly captivated by her contradictions.

'You could always come and lie next to me,' he suggested helpfully. He flicked an invisible speck of dust from his trousers and said casually, 'You can't avoid the bed, you know.' He patted the space next to him. 'I'll talk to you about it if you'd just relax a little.'

With a fuming, strangled sound, Ruth shut the bedroom door and then leant heavily against it.

You can't avoid the bed. Did he think that she imagined, for one minute, that she *could*? When it engulfed the entire room and made looking at anything else within those four small walls an impossibility?

'I am very relaxed,' Ruth informed him stiffly, and he grinned at her.

'If your fingers dig any harder into your sides, you'll rip your clothing.'

Ruth refused to see anything funny in his remark. She didn't know what game he was playing, whether he was inspired by some sick desire for revenge just because she had had the temerity to walk out on him, but she wasn't going to stand for it. Her hands might be tied, but that didn't mean that she was going to let him get away with murder.

'Just answer me,' she said through gritted teeth.

'When you calm down.' He swung his long legs over the side of the bed and stood up, stretching. Then he began to undo the buttons of his shirt.

'What are you doing?'

'What does it look like I'm doing?'

Ruth gulped. In many ways it would have been easier if she had never seen him naked before. As it was, her mind could provide her with all the tantalising and accurate details about his body, well muscled, hard and lithe. She had traced its contours with her fingers often enough to know how helpless the sight of it would make her feel. She shifted her eyes away and maintained a lofty silence.

'I'm going to have a bath,' he said mildly. 'The drive from London was a nightmare.' He stripped off his shirt, rummaged in one of the two suitcases he had lugged up with him, and extracted a white dressing gown of the expensive hotel variety.

She had never seen him in a dressing gown before. Nudity was something he was not uncomfortable with, and when they had been lovers he had enjoyed her watching his nakedness as much as she had enjoyed doing it.

'Care to come? I could soap you.' He threw her a long, slow smile. 'You've always enjoyed that.' His voice was low and husky, and in spite of herself she felt her body begin to stir at the memory.

Another fractional tilt of the head gave him the answer to that one, but, although she looked away, she could still see him out of the corner of her eye as he shrugged off the work shirt and then the trousers and finally his boxer shorts.

Oh, *God*. Ruth licked her lips. Every muscle in her body, every pore and vein and blood vessel seemed to be stretched to breaking point, and a fine film of perspiration had broken out over her entire body.

'Do you remember?' He took a couple of steps in her direction, and, with alarm, she realised that the dressing gown had still not been donned. He had it hooked over one shoulder.

'No!' Her head was now at a right angle, but the bedroom was so small that she couldn't help *but* see his magnificent body. Nor could she fail to notice his flagrant arousal.

'Of course you do,' he said in a silky persuasive voice. He was now standing close enough to her that if she reached out a couple of inches she would bump into him. 'You'd climb into the bath, luxuriate in the water and *I would*...'

'Ruth promptly covered her ears with her hands and squeezed her eyes tightly shut.

'I would...'

She felt his hands cover hers and gently prise them away from her ears.

'I would soap you all over, starting with your feet, massaging the soles so that you'd sink a little deeper into the water, and then...'

'I'm not interested!' Ruth said breathlessly. She couldn't help but hear him, but she refused to open her eyes and see him as well.

'Oh, yes, you are. I know you a damn sight better than you think and I know when your mouth is saying one thing and everything else is screaming something entirely different.' He leaned a little closer and spoke into her ear. 'You used to laugh because your legs would be unsteady when you finally stood up so that I could finish my job, so that I could work the soap into a foaming, warm lather and then I'd...'

'Shut up!'

'Are you getting turned on?'

'No, I'm not.'

'Then I'd soap your breasts, full, slippery breasts...your nipples would be hard and you'd have your head thrown back as if you were offering them to my mouth, holding them out to be suckled.'

He took one crucial step closer and his hard arousal pressed against her thighs.

Ruth was finding it remarkably easy to remember just how wobbly her legs had used to feel when she'd tried to stand up in that bath. Much the same as they were feeling right now. She pressed herself back against the door, breathing rapidly.

'And then,' he murmured into her ear, holding her head with his hand so that she couldn't escape him, 'I would work the soap over your stomach. Remember? Over your stomach and down to your thighs...'

'No. Stop. Please.'

'And between them. Slowly and thoroughly. Between your thighs, and then I would touch you where you were aching to be touched, and rub you there, and there would be no telling where your natural dampness and the bath water began... Are you wet for me now?' He laughed softly, and then flicked his tongue into her ear so that she moaned and squirmed at the same time. 'Can I feel? Find out if you're as turned on as I am?'

His voice was mesmerising. There was no other word for it. She had been hypnotised, or at least that was how she felt. He undid the button of her jeans and then pulled down the zip. From a great distance, she seemed to be watching all of this, and to be incapable of stopping it.

He pushed his hand beneath her underwear and then, what she had been waiting for, every nerve stretched to breaking point, his finger slid inexorably into her, rubbing against the dainty bud, now swollen with pleasure, circling and pressing it until she thought she might go mad with desire.

Stripped of sanity, she found herself shakily unbuttoning her shirt, easing her breasts out of her bra without bothering to unclasp it at the back, and she watched, fascinated, as his mouth found her engorged nipple and he began tugging at it, pulling it into his mouth while his tongue rasped against the tender, swollen bud.

'Enjoying this, darling?'

Ruth nodded. In a minute she would concentrate on the stupidity of her actions. Right now his mouth and fingers were doing crazy things to her nervous system, crazy things she thought she might be addicted to.

'Why fight what we feel for one another?' he whispered, straightening to kiss her while his fingers continued to play with her moist, feminine cavity. 'We still want one another. Why stop it? Why not just see where it leads?'

Ruth drowsily considered his question, and when she opened her eyes it was to find him looking at her urgently.

'Accept this,' he said. 'Let's enjoy one another.'

His words were like a gush of cold water over her. He wanted her to enjoy what they had, but even now she could feel her own enjoyment fading and her erotic oblivion being swiftly replaced by dawning horror that she had been so happy to jeopardise her peace of mind for the sake of a few moments of stolen pleasure. She pulled away sharply.

'Stop fighting me,' he said. 'Why fight? Why wage war when we can make love? Why struggle when we both want to give in?'

'Because giving in to what we felt for one another was what landed us in this mess.' She risked opening her eyes to look at him.

'Lying to your parents is what landed us in this mess.'

'And how would it have been any different otherwise?' Ruth demanded, finding her strength now that she wasn't having the ground yanked away from under her by the seductive lure of his voice with all its erotic fantasies. She had squirmed totally out of his grasp and was shakily redressing herself.

He clicked his tongue and stuck on the ubiquitous dressing gown.

'If you'd said something from the start…'

'How could I?' she asked hotly. 'Neither of us had planned on a baby. Are you telling me that you would have been over the moon if I'd sat you down and informed you that you were going to be a daddy?'

Yes. The tiny word crept into his head with shocking effect. He stared at her and his mind had gone completely and utterly blank. Blank but for that single admission that had stolen into his brain without giving the slightest forewarning of its intent.

Taking his silence for agreement, Ruth felt her anger gather momentum.

'You would have been horrified!' she said, hugging herself tightly as he pulled the robe around him and gazed down at her belligerently. 'You say that you know me better than I think. Well, *I* know *you* better than *you* think! You've lived your life this far without managing to be snagged by anyone and that's the way you like it. You've made no bones about that! Did you think that I was the sort of girl to push you into a role of responsibility you had neither courted nor wanted? Would you have appreciated the gesture?'

Ruth couldn't believe that she was raging at this man with a furious eloquence that she had never had at her command before. He had given her strength without even knowing. Just one more thing, she thought bitterly, to be lost in the rubble of their relationship, one more good thing to spend the rest of her days remembering.

Franco continued to stare at her in silence as he grappled with his own line of thought which, having taken root, now seemed to be growing at a frightening rate.

So this was what it felt like to have the shoe on the other foot. A ridiculous situation, of which he had zero experience, had come home to roost with a vengeance.

Ruth might well have done what she did for misguided but naïvely altruistic reasons. How ironic that he now found himself in the position of craving the one thing she didn't want. Stability, commitment. He couldn't bring himself to say the *Marriage* word, not even to himself.

'Well? *Well?* Are you going to answer me?' she pressed on bitterly. There was the glimmer of tears in the corners of her eyes and she wiped them away with an exasperated gesture.

'You make it sound as though I intend to swan through life as a bachelor so that I can die a lonely old man, because picking women up and dumping them is what I enjoy doing...'

'Let's be honest,' Ruth said painfully, looking away from him. 'Even if you *were* to get married, at some point in the future, later rather than sooner, then it wouldn't be to someone like me. Just because I'm a country bumpkin doesn't mean that I'm the village idiot as well. I *know* the kind of woman you would be attracted to, the kind of woman you would want by your side, and I don't fit the bill.' She gave a short, choked laugh. 'I'm not polished, I don't possess all those sophisticated little ways, I blush too much!'

'That's a load of nonsense. You…'

'Don't, Franco,' she said wearily. 'What's happened has happened. All we can do is accept it now, but if sleeping with you is part of your end of the deal, part of the deal for agreeing to keep my parents in the dark about the reality of the situation, then, thanks but no thanks.'

'How the hell can you talk about making love together as a *deal*?' He shook his head and raked his fingers through his hair. 'What kind of man do you think I am, for God's sake? The sort who would try and blackmail you into bed?'

'I didn't mean that,' Ruth objected, confused because her words had been misinterpreted somewhere along the way. There was nothing sleazy about Franco, but without thinking she had made him sound that way.

'Don't worry,' he said harshly, 'you can sleep peacefully in the bed tonight. I won't lay a finger on you. And in the morning I'll be gone.'

His words went straight to her heart like a sliver of glass.

'There's no need,' she began weakly.

'Correction. There's *every* need. And you needn't worry that I'll spill the beans to your parents. They, at any rate, deserve better than that. No, I'll do the vanishing act you were so desperate for me to do and then I shall make contact with you via a lawyer.

Know this, though—I will *not* vanish out of my child's life, and I don't care *how much* that will suit you. I *will* see the baby and you *will* accept mainte-nance for yourself and for the child. What you do with yours is your affair, but no child of mine will ever want for anything.

'Now—' he nodded to the door against which she seemed adhered as though with glue '—if you don't mind, I'll go and have my bath. Where you sleep is your concern, but I shall be sleeping on that bed. Take it or leave it.'

Ruth stood aside silently to let him pass, and when she heard the click of the bathroom door further down the corridor she felt her body sag, as though invisible strings holding it up had suddenly been severed.

Now that she was getting what she wanted, she real-ised what she had known all along. She didn't want it. She never had. She didn't want Franco to do a con-venient vanishing act, and she didn't want her com-munications with him to be reduced to conversations between lawyers.

But there was a big difference between what she wanted, what she could have and what had been of-fered, and Ruth knew that, however tempting it was to snatch at the little she had on the off chance that it might lead to bigger, more substantial things, she would be a fool to do it.

She undressed and slipped into her nightie, the starched maiden aunt one, and then crept along the corridor to the unused bathroom, which was the size of a matchbox, and up a few winding stairs *en route* to the attic. There, she washed her face, brushed her teeth and then rested on the sink and stared at her reflection in the mirror.

Looking for changes in her body had become something of a nightly ritual. After she had recovered from the initial shock of her pregnancy, a deep feeling of satisfied pleasure had taken its place. She had become accustomed to inspecting her face and her body for any differences. Her breasts, she knew, had grown. She had never been flat-chested and now they were heavy, the nipples bigger and darker than before.

Her stomach was beginning to fill out too, though not obviously so. She just fitted into her clothes a little more snugly. Soon those small changes would become unmistakable, until her stomach would swell with her child, *their* child.

Knowing that Franco would not be around to witness any of those changes was like carrying a splinter around in her heart.

Knowing that he would share their child but not her life was an ache that seemed to have no end.

Worse than that was the knowledge that one day he would meet a woman with whom he wanted to build his life, and it would be inevitable that she, Ruth, would meet this woman, would know that the happiness *she* would never have belonged to someone else, and she would have to smile bravely through that knowledge even if she was weeping inside.

It was scant comfort to know that she was doing the right thing in standing firm against Franco. She had already paid dearly for giving in to temptation. She placed the flat of her hand against her stomach and stood very, very still, wondering if she could feel the baby move inside her. But it was too early yet, and, with a little sigh, she headed back towards the bedroom.

Evidence of Franco's decision to leave was strewn around the room. A pile of clothing lay on the bed and his two suitcases had been dragged out and opened. More clothes were crammed in, a creased bundle of shirts, trousers, underwear, ties and socks.

Ruth watched numbly as he continued to hurl more various items of clothing from bed to case, ignoring her in the process.

'There's no need for you to leave tonight,' she said weakly, and when he didn't bother to look at her, she repeated herself in a louder voice.

'But isn't that what you *want*?' Franco jeered, flinging some aftershave into the case with venomous precision. He was wearing a pair of khaki-coloured trousers and a shirt which had not been buttoned up and gaped to expose the muscular wall of his chest.

Yes, he admitted with vicious self-disgust, he had finally reached the bottom of the road. Here he was, self-control shot to hell, acting like a toddler. And *she* was to blame. She of the creamy hair and creamy skin and innocent, dreamy smile that could drive a man mad within seconds. She had reduced him to *this*. Pelting clothes into a suitcase glowering with rage and confusion and sheer, bloody *hurt*.

He looked at her, standing by the door, her face wearing an appalled expression, and a lifetime of knowing precisely what to say on precisely what occasion deserted him. He knew that if he opened his mouth he would not be able to hide his bewilderment at this strange turn of the tide.

'It's for the best,' she said miserably. 'But there's no need for you to…to be so dramatic… I mean…'

'*Dramatic?*' His voice was thick with an ominous tone of threat, and Ruth looked at him hesitantly. Of course she had said the wrong thing. Didn't she specialise in that? It was only natural that he would be furious at her refusal to go along with him. He was a sophisticated man of the world. He would be utterly perplexed at the moral inconsistency of a woman who could happily sleep with him until she got pregnant, and then wouldn't come within a mile of him.

'I d-didn't mean *dramatic*…' she stammered.

The accuracy of the description had cut to the quick. He *was*, he knew, being dramatic. Behaving like a complete ass. And the worst of it was that he just couldn't help himself. His hand was throwing items of clothing into the suitcase, the muscles in his face were contracting into an expression of glowering rage, his mouth appeared to have a will of its own and was spouting forth the sort of rubbish that he would have sneered at in someone else.

And where the hell was his brain in all of this? His brain was fine, thank you very much. His *brain* knew full well that he should just walk away from the situation and give her what she craved, namely his absence, even though her body might still want to be touched by his.

'Mum and Dad are going to wonder… I mean, we've… *you've* only just gone and bought…' She gestured towards the bed, which had been the source of this final, tragic showdown. 'What are they going to think?'

'It's time you stopped living for what your parents

want,' he said harshly, snapping shut the suitcases and buttoning up his shirt.

'I don't *live* for what my parents want.' Ruth took a deep breath and lashed out with unexpected vigour. 'I consider their feelings. That's something entirely different. Haven't *you* ever considered the feelings of someone else?'

There was a telling silence, then Ruth said slowly, 'You haven't, have you? You've always had what you wanted. You have money and charm and good looks and...and...everything's always gone your way. You've never *had* to stand back and think about other people because other people were always there, thinking about *you*.'

'That's a load of rubbish,' he countered uncomfortably, wondering how her description of him as having charm and good looks had managed to backfire into an insult.

'No, it's not. It's the truth.' She took a few steps into the room, stepping around the suitcases and heading for the small wooden rocking chair that was now jammed against the wall since the arrival of the double bed. She sat down and looked at him.

'That's why you're in such a rush to get out of here. You wanted to sleep with me and because I said no, you decided to clear out as fast as your legs could take you. Now that you won't be getting what you want, you no longer feel the need to impress Mum and Dad, or even to tell them to their face that you're leaving. You've washed your hands of the situation and you can't wait to clear out.'

'Listen to yourself!' His voice was confidently dismissive, but he still had to admit to himself that what she had said made sense, even if every single word was wildly off target. 'I'm doing what *you* want and you have the nerve to tell me that I'm being inconsiderate!'

'I'm asking you to wait until morning, at least. You've gone and told Mum and Dad that...' She could feel her eyes welling up again, and she gulped back the urge to cry. Hormones, pregnancy and a naturally soft nature were conspiring to turn her into a sodden, weeping mess. 'That a blessing would be a brilliant idea, and now, just when they will have gone to bed crowing with delight at the thought of it, planning what needs to be done, you're prepared to walk out without even saying goodbye!'

'I...' Now he felt like a cad. For once in his life he had been propelled by emotion, and he had come out of it looking like a cad. He shot her a seething, defensive look, but was finding it difficult to defend his stance.

'Not that I knew what possessed you to go along with the idea in the first place,' she swept on, caught on an unstoppable current of recrimination. 'Things are complicated enough without them being further complicated!'

'I...'

'Will *you let me finish?'* The ferocity of her command threw him for six, and he literally took a step backwards before looking at her narrowly, the amusement back in his eyes as he absorbed the quivering angel in front of him.

He wasn't going to let her go. He was *never* going to let her go. And if she didn't love him, then she would learn to. Because she was the only woman he had ever loved and the only one he ever would. He would use the physical hold he knew he had over her and he would work until her defences were broken.

The decision left him with a feeling of calm. Let her rant and rave; her fate was sealed. He was her fate just as she was his, and his pride was not going to stand in the way of something as big and overwhelming and wonderful as this.

'So now you just intend to walk away and leave *me* to pick up the pieces behind you…!'

'Well, there would be no pieces to pick up if it weren't for you in the first place…'

'There's no point harking on about what was done…'

'Why are you so against the idea of a blessing, anyway?' Franco asked, swerving away from the topic of his departure, which appeared more pointless and rash as the minutes ticked by.

'Because it doesn't seem *right*,' Ruth muttered, angling her body up to him.

'It's no less *right* than the fictitious marriage we're supposed to be enjoying!' he bit back with grim logic.

'You know what I mean,' Ruth was obliged to counteract stubbornly, and he shook his head in wonderment, as though thoroughly bemused by her illogic.

'No, I don't! I don't damn well know what you mean! And I'm sick to death and utterly fed up with all of this!' *Where was he going with this?*

He stalked across to the suitcase and began pelting clothes out, back onto the bed, where they collected into a hideously untidy mound. Her mouth had dropped open, which was mildly satisfying.

'I'm staying! Do you hear me? I'm not going anywhere? I'm in love with you and you'll damn well accept that and start loving me back if it's the last thing you do!'

As a declaration of devotion, he was forced to admit it left a great deal to be desired, but he was beyond caring.

'And will you stop looking at me as though I've turned into a three-headed alien? You're pregnant with *my* child...' even in the midst of his roaring anger he couldn't prevent a note of pride from creeping into his voice '...and if you think that you're going to selfishly waltz out of my life now, then you're wrong! We're man and wife—'

'But we're not *really*...' Ruth interrupted meekly.

'Well, we *will be*! We're getting married. We're going to be a family! Do you understand me?'

'Because you love me?' She gazed at him, adoring the sullen lines of his mouth and loving him for the strength she knew it must have taken for him to broadcast his feelings when he was uncertain of the response.

'Yes,' he muttered grimly.

'Adore me, even?'

A slow smile began to tug the corners of his mouth. 'Even that,' he agreed.

'Would worship be too big a word?'

'Not big enough...'

Ruth smiled. 'Ditto.'

CHAPTER TEN

RUTH felt as though she was swimming. Swimming up to the surface of the water, where she would be able to take a huge gulp of air and breathe again. That would have been very nice, were it not for the fact that she didn't want to regain consciousness. She couldn't quite think why, but she knew that floating around in her present dreamlike state was infinitely better than waking up to reality.

She opened her eyes tentatively to find Franco staring down at her. She was lying on a bed in a very small room with white walls and a television inappropriately set on brackets against the wall. Around her was a scrunched-up mass of white sheets. Fear and panic flooded her, and she felt the desire to cry well up inside her like an unstoppable tidal wave.

In the space of a few seconds everything, every emotion, every word and every thought, came back to her with nightmarish clarity.

She had been standing in the finished nursery at their newly bought London mews house. Her parents had been deeply impressed because all the decorating had been contracted out to professionals. Someone had come in and, in the space of a week, had turned the high-ceilinged room with the gorgeous bay window into a wonderful green and yellow nursery.

Of course Ruth had muttered about the expense, through sheer habit, and Franco had squashed her re-

luctance with raised eyebrows and an amused, teasing
remark about the impossibility of climbing ladders and
hanging wallpaper when her stomach was the size of
a large beachball.

'It's decadent.' She had grinned back at him with a
sigh. 'You're a very, very decadent man, and I'm surprised the local vicar gave you his blessing to be involved with me.'

'The local vicar,' he had murmured seductively,
'has no idea how deliciously decadent his daughter can
be when the mood takes her. Or, for that matter, how
often the mood *does* take her!'

At that point in time, with the sunshine streaming
through the window and with only five weeks of her
pregnancy left to go, there had been no clouds on the
horizon.

No clouds, at least, until she had felt the rapid onset
of contractions when none were yet due. She had made
it to the telephone, even as her waters had broken, and
had managed to get through to Emergency, but Franco
had been at a meeting in the depths of Wiltshire and
she had had to leave a breathless and urgent message
with his secretary.

The worst thing she remembered were the ominous
words, *The baby's showing signs of distress. We'll
have to perform a Caesarean.* To her untrained ears
that had sounded like a death sentence on her baby,
and the anaesthetic delivered to knock her out had
come as a blessing.

'Ruth...' Franco began, now leaning towards her,
and she turned her head away and bit her lip.

'No, don't say it. Please don't say it.'

'You silly girl.' When he lifted his hand to stroke

her hair she could feel it trembling, and she looked at him. His face was haggard. He looked as though he hadn't slept for a week.

'The baby...' She found that she couldn't get the words out properly. The rest of the unfinished sentence stuck somewhere at the back of her throat and she had to rely on her pleading, tear-filled eyes to complete what her mouth could not say.

'Is in the Special Case Unit.' He smiled at her, and Ruth closed her eyes and felt her entire body go limp with relief. The relief, however, was short-lived. 'We had a girl, my darling, and she's beautiful.'

'Are you sure?' Ruth whispered. Was he lying? Was he lying because he felt that she was too weak for the truth? She looked straight into his eyes, anxiously trying to prise the truth out of him, and he kissed her on her forehead.

'I think I know enough to recognise the difference between a boy and a girl.'

'I know, but you *know* what I mean...'

'She's absolutely fine, Ruth. Small, but the doctors have said that there's no reason why we shouldn't be able to take her home in the next couple of weeks. She just needs a bit of feeding up, and they want to make sure that her lungs are functioning to full capacity before they let her go.' He kissed the corner of her mouth. 'They'll be in to tell you all this themselves in a little while, and as soon as you're up to it we'll go and have a peep at her.'

'Mum and Dad...?'

'Know, and are on their way down.' He exhaled a long, shaky breath, squeezed shut his eyes, and when he re-opened them they were suspiciously shiny.

'Don't ever scare me like that again, Ruthie,' he said unsteadily. 'I want to tell you this before the doctors arrive and I'm shooed out.

'When Caroline interrupted me in that meeting and told me that there had been a little hiccup and the baby was on its way, I think I felt my heart stop beating.' He laughed drily under his breath and looked at her.

'This may come as a shock—you *know* what a calm, placid, accepting person I am...' to which Ruth couldn't help but chuckle with tender denial '...but I was quite a boor with the driver, who stupidly seemed to attract every traffic jam and red light between Winchester and London and idiotically couldn't turn his car into a hovercraft.

'Then I was even more of a boor when I got here...demanding to be told what was going on...accosting every nurse on the ward for updates on how you were doing in the operating thea-tre...virtually asking for the surgeon's references to be shown to me...I'm fairly surprised that they treated me as indulgently as they did...'

'I've been in perfectly good hands,' Ruth chided, thrilled with his confession, though he hardly needed to tell her, because after all those months she was *to-tally secure* in her knowledge of how much this won-derful man improbably adored her. 'Now, tell me all about her. Does she have any hair?'

'Not much, I'm afraid. She's very tiny, but she has the loveliest long fingers.' He seemed to be struggling to find the right words and Ruth smiled at him.

By the time she was robed and walking, supported by Franco, with her parents behind them, to the Special Care ward where her daughter was, Ruth had heard enough of her little miracle of creation from Franco to write several books on the subject. Fatherhood, the one thing he had steadfastly avoided until he had found himself without option, appeared to have turned him into a doting, boringly proud dad.

'There she is,' he said proudly, pointing to a little sleeping beauty, and Ruth smiled and looked around at her parents.

'She looks just like you,' her mother said, smiling. 'Let's hope she's not as demanding!'

One year later…and as Ruth lay on the beach, with her head resting on Franco's shoulder and his arm thrown carelessly around her, she felt his free hand creep suggestively across the taut contours of her stomach.

'Are you *mad*?' She giggled and looked around her, but at a little after eleven in the night the beach was empty of people. The silvery moonlight made the surface of the tropical sea turn to glass and behind them the rustle of coconut trees was the only sound to be heard. That, and the steady lapping of ocean against shore.

'Why not? How many honeymoons do a couple have?'

'Depends how many times they get married,' Ruth said sensibly, and she smiled as his arm tightened around her.

'In our case, then. One honeymoon.' He nibbled her ear and blew into it, sending an erotic thrill through her. 'And we have ten long, lazy, Natasha-free days to enjoy it just how we want to, and if that includes making love on the beach at midnight, then why not?'

The free hand slipped beneath her shirt and found the full swell of her breast, unrestricted by a bra. He cupped the soft mound and then rubbed her nipple with the pad of his finger until it jutted into hard arousal. With a sigh of pleasure Ruth stretched out, raising her arms above her, all the better to enjoy the feel of his hands on her body.

He was right. Natasha was back in England, being looked after by her adoring grandparents, who, from virtually the minute she had arrived at the vicarage for a visit, were insisting on taking her to do the rounds of the parishioners.

And Natasha seemed to love the attention. She had left the hospital at two weeks, still small and hairless, and now, at the end of a year, possessed some very sturdy limbs, a headful of pale golden hair and cornflower-blue eyes that were fringed by the same dark lashes as her father's.

'But what if someone comes along?' Ruth whispered half-heartedly, revelling in the flash of Franco's possessive, hungry eyes. She sighed as he slowly began undoing the buttons of her shirt.

Even at this hour it was warm enough to be wearing only a short-sleeved shirt and a pair of shorts. Underneath them, the giant-sized beach spread was a scant but effective barrier against the pale sand, and as the last of the buttons on her shirt was undone Ruth wriggled sensuously, closing her eyes and waiting for that moment when she would feel the wetness of his mouth enclose her throbbing nipple.

She arched herself up a bit and shuddered as the moment arrived and his tongue flicked across the sensitive peaks, followed by his mouth as he began suckling hard on the protruding buds, taking them one at a time until she was lost in a world of sensation.

Her fingers curled into his dark hair and she moaned when he started tugging down her elasticised shorts. He knew her body so well, and yet it never failed to amaze her that he could still turn her on with the same deep, greedy need that she had felt the very first time he had laid a finger on her.

She dropped her knees to either side and his eager, determined fingers slipped beneath her briefs, unswervingly finding the little soft spot and the core of her femininity, gently rubbing it while her body responded with moist approval.

If a hundred spectators came along now, there would be nothing she could do to stop the waves of pleasure engulfing her and her need to go to the final place of fulfilment. He trailed his tongue along her stomach, which had fortunately tightened back into shape, although its contours were slightly more rounded and womanly than before, while his fingers continued to idly tease her pulsating womanhood.

Her underwear was damp when he finally removed it, so that he could press her thighs against the sand, spreading wide her legs and settling between them to enjoy the mysterious, intensely feminine dampness between.

Ruth moaned as his tongue slid through the furry, downy patch of hair, carving a path to that beating centre of excitement. She tilted her body upwards and rotated her hips while his mouth became greedier, enjoying her writhing body with the appetite of the gourmand feasting upon an exquisitely prepared meal.

Before she could reach the pinnacle of fulfilment,

however, Franco raised his head, allowing her frantic craving to abate, giving him time to slip off his shorts and guide his thick, hard arousal deep into her.

He moved slowly at first, enjoying the way she moved and wriggled, wanting him to speed up his tempo so that she could reach orgasm.

He teased her all the time about being a vicar's daughter, yet also being the most wanton, abandoned woman in bed he had ever known, but, however many positions they sampled, this was still the one he liked most. His body over hers. Like this, he could look down and feast his eyes on the vision of her breasts, bouncing as she twisted under him, the nipples larger and darker now than they had been before she became pregnant.

Sometimes he stilled them with his hands, loving the feel of their softness, enjoying the sensation of massaging them and kneading them until her nipples seemed even more engorged and swollen pushing upwards, offering themselves to his mouth.

Most of all, however, he just enjoyed watching her face, her eyes shut, her nostrils flaring as he brought her closer and faster to her climax.

It seemed as though he could never tire of this bewitching woman who had borne his child and who, with the flicker of an eye, could still turn his muscles to jelly.

Work, the thing he had lived and died for, had faded into a paltry second best to his wife and child. Meals out on a nightly basis had become an intrusion into what he wanted most to do—namely, get home as early as he could, in time to see something of his daughter. And then, when she had gone to sleep, to enjoy his wife's home-cooked food and the deeply re-laxing, wonderfully satisfying conversations they had. No high-powered banter with clients could come close to watching her blush or giggle or just look at him with her wide grey eyes.

He felt the salty film of her perspiration mixing with his, and for a fleeting second he closed his eyes and pushed deep into her, opening them to gaze at her face as she emitted a long, satisfied groan and he felt his own life force seep out of him and flood her body.

Would it be ridiculous, he wondered, if he told her *thank you*?

One month later, and with Natasha sound asleep in her cot, Ruth curled her body into Franco's, drawing up her legs and resting her head against his chest. She could hear his heart beating in this position and there was something foolishly comforting about that.

His feet were stretched out on the table in front of them, and on the television a blonde presenter was winding up the news with a touching, sentimental story of some endangered animal or other in a zoo somewhere or other.

Ruth didn't really hear what was being said. She had been waiting for this moment all evening, enjoy-ing the thrill of anticipation as they ate their dinner, chatted and touched and chatted and touched again, their minds and bodies perfectly in tune with one an-other.

'Oh, by the way,' she said, stretching and sitting up straight so that she could see his face, 'a bit of news.'

He smiled slowly at her. 'Seeing that you've left it

this late, I know it's got to be important. Not to do with the retreat, is it?'

That was their code name for the house they were buying in the country, not five miles away from the vicarage—somewhere they could escape to on the occasional weekend when they weren't seeing friends.

'Don't tell me that half-wit estate agent's screwed up.' He frowned, anticipating unwelcome news. The cottage, derelict though it was, had limitless potential, and if they lost it he would personally hang the little twit by the feet from the nearest available tree. He had done precious little to secure the deal in the first place.

'No, no, no,' Ruth said hastily, seeing the warning signs from her husband, who could still intimidate when he chose and whose appreciation of the estate agent handling the matter had been reduced to rubble when he'd caught the hapless boy sneaking furtive glances at his wife.

'What, then? Come back here, where you were sitting. I liked being able to put my hand just there, on your left breast.'

'In a minute,' Ruth told him, determined not to be side-tracked, even though the prospect of his hand caressing her breast was almost too tempting to resist. 'I want to see your face when I break this to you…'

'Break what?'

Ruth took a deep breath and said, in a pleased rush, 'You're going to be a father for a second time!' His reaction was everything she had hoped: surprise very quickly followed by delight. 'I *think*,' she added, 'that a certain night spent on a certain beach when a certain man couldn't keep his hands off me is to blame for that.'

'Oh, is that right?' he murmured softly, the strong, aggressive contours of his face softened by his smile. 'All I can say to that, Mrs Leoni, is that it worked...'

'What did?'

'Well...' He pulled her toward him and returned his hand to the place he wanted it to be, covering the mound of her breast, then he kissed the top of her head. 'My plan for Natasha to have a baby brother or sister...' He pulled down the straps of her vest-style tee shirt to expose the breast he had been caressing, soft and full, the big nipple ripe with expectation of the baby growing inside his wife.

'Does that mean...' Ruth lowered her eyes and smiled a secret smile '...that now your dastardly plan has succeeded there'll be no more rehearsals for that baby brother or sister?' She lay back against the arm of the sofa and pulled the vest down to her waist, watching as his eyes glittered in appreciation of her body.

'Typical female!' he growled, bending to nuzzle her soft skin. 'No logic at all...'

Ruth closed her eyes and sighed. How was it that her parents had never told her that heaven was something you could touch...?

VIVA LA VIDA DE AMOR!

They speak the language of passion.

In Harlequin Presents®, you'll find a special
kind of lover—full of Latin charm. Whether
he's relaxing in denims or dressed for dinner,
giving you diamonds or simply sweet dreams,
he's got spirit, style and sex appeal!

Latin Lovers is the new miniseries
from Harlequin Presents® for anyone
who enjoys hot romance!

Meet gorgeous Antonio Scarlatti in
THE BLACKMAILED BRIDEGROOM
by Miranda Lee, Harlequin Presents® #2151
available January 2001

And don't miss sexy Niccolo Dominici in
THE ITALIAN GROOM
by Jane Porter, Harlequin Presents® #2168
available March 2001!

Available wherever Harlequin books are sold.

He's a man of cool sophistication.
He's got pride, power and wealth.
He's a ruthless businessman, an expert lover—
and he's one hundred percent committed
to staying single.

Until now. Because suddenly he's responsible
for a BABY!

HIS BABY

An exciting miniseries from Harlequin Presents®
**He's sexy, he's successful...
and now he's facing up to fatherhood!**

On sale February 2001:
RAFAEL'S LOVE-CHILD
by Kate Walker, Harlequin Presents® #2160

On sale May 2001:
MORGAN'S SECRET SON
by Sara Wood, Harlequin Presents® #2180

And look out for more later in the year!

Available wherever Harlequin books are sold.

**Lindsay Armstrong...
Helen Bianchin...
Emma Darcy...
Miranda Lee...**

Some of our bestselling writers are Australians!

Look our for their novels about the Wonder from Down Under—where spirited women win the hearts of Australia's most eligible men.

THE AUSTRALIANS

Coming soon:

THE MARRIAGE RISK
by Emma Darcy
On sale February 2001, Harlequin Presents® #2157

And look out for:

MARRIAGE AT A PRICE
by Miranda Lee
On sale June 2001, Harlequin Presents® #2181

Available wherever Harlequin books are sold.

HARLEQUIN®
Makes any time special ™